THE MAN WHO INVENTED WRITING

Baker Lawley

This is a work of fiction. Names, places, businesses, characters and incidents are either the product of the author's imagination or are used in a fictitious manner. Any resemblance to actual persons living or dead, actual events or actual locales is entirely coincidental.

Cover image courtesy
kuradamon.deviantart.com

ISBN: 0615724140
ISBN-13: 978-0615724140

This book is dedicated
to all storytellers
and all the ways
stories are told.

Contents

FOREWORD

Over and over, the earth spins in the same orbit. Seasons come and pass, the sun rises and sets.

And when a new idea appears, it changes nothing. Not at first. Everything feels much the same as always.

But if it is good enough, the idea takes root. Slowly, like the seasons, the new thing grows until it is as natural as a sunrise and a sunset.

And as always, the world spins, seasons come and pass, and nobody can imagine what it was like before the idea was there.

This is the story of how the world is changed. One new idea at a time.

This is the story of when a great people began to live in a world of new ideas.

They were living in a great peace, the first in many generations.

So these nomadic people settled in place. They built huts with walls and roofs that protected them from the elements. They lived in tight groups for protection and cooperation. They foraged and hunted together, gathered water to share.

And they told stories.

As the world spun and the seasons passed, the stories were always changing, growing new limbs like young trees, blooming new flowers with each new telling.

When artists tried to capture the stories with carvings and paintings on rock faces and tortoise shells, they were always too late. By the time they depicted it, the story had changed.

For they lived in a time when there was no way to make a story permanent. There was no system to record them. Stories existed only as thoughts in the people's minds, words made only of sounds in the air.

And all along in this time of peace, when a people began living by one new idea, then another, and another, the stories changed so many times they became legends.

And those legends became the foundation of a great culture.

This is the story of a legend, about the man who found a way to make the stories permanent.

This is the story of the man who invented writing.

This is the story of how writing changed the world.

The Messenger's Burden

It was early in the morning, or perhaps late at night, or somewhere so far within its own darkness that the world could just fold in on itself and tell no more stories, when a small noise—a tiny twig breaking, a roof beam settling against its wall—woke Cangjie in his bed. The slightest noises did this to him, and probably would forever. He lay there, his heart thudding and his mind alert, and he sighed.

Now that the wars had ended and Cangjie slept each night under his own safe roof, there was no reason for him to be so alarmed any longer. He tried to settle back on his mat, reminding himself that this world he lived in was entirely new, and his life no longer depended on hearing the smallest sounds of his enemy.

As his heart slowed, Cangjie's mind drifted back to past times. Before now, he had lived in a time of great unrest, as had all of his ancestors. Cangjie knew the story of how, in times past, his tribe had come to ally with others under their leader, the Yellow Emperor. He almost smiled to remember himself as a young man, idealistic and seeking adventure, when he had joined his Emperor's army as they gathered against the threat of the invading Yan Emperor of Shennong.

In his years of fighting, Cangjie had proven himself lithe and slippery, as difficult to catch as a bat or a breeze, with a memory like the strongest netting. He'd become the most trusted messenger of his commander, and because of his skill with words and messages and his knack for escaping capture, Cangjie had risen up through the ranks of the Yellow Emperor's army. He spent years traveling the land in stealth, carrying secrets in his mind and delivering them to powerful superiors in the army who knew what to do with them.

Cangjie's messages, he knew back then, were crucial. It was because of him that the armies were prepared for many battles against the Shennong.

As he lay awake there in the dark, his thoughts wandering in times long past, Cangjie let the brutal memories of fighting in the three great battles of Banquan stay as nothing more than vague feelings, whispers and spirits in his mind.

Instead, Cangjie remembered the surprise he felt when Yandi surrendered after those terrible battles, and they were all united as the Huaxia tribe, and the bodies of his commanders were discovered, dead on the field of battle.

Cangjie had thus become the Yellow Emperor's Master of Communications.

Even now, all these years later, safe in his home in the dark morning, he still could not believe he had risen to a rank so high.

Cangjie listened to other noises from the outside

world, no longer fearing an assassin's footstep or an ambush. He could not stop his mind from telling his own story to himself again.

He remembered that, soon after this great victory, they learned of the Juili tribe's advances toward their territories, and the jealousy of their leader, Chi You. As Master of Communications, Cangjie had been burdened with great responsibility and great knowledge.

His messengers and spies brought him information and prisoners, and deep in the forest Cangjie had done terrible things for more information. He burned the bottom of men's feet to torture words from them, and left them there to be eaten by dragons. He skinned Juili scouts alive to hear what they knew. As he watched the flies swarming on their raw muscles, he heard also their pleas for merciful death to Kui Xing, god of examinations. He witnessed their mad fear as they saw creatures Cangjie and his men could not—the Pixiu like a winged lion, the mountain demon Xiao. Then Cangjie sent messages to the Yellow Emperor and his generals of what he'd learned from these dying men.

Cangjie knew he had done horrible things to men who were really not that different from himself. But their words helped the Yellow Emperor and the Huaxia tribe defeat Chi You soundly at the Battle of Zhoulu.

And then, peace. It was as strange as if the seasons had stopped turning, for now there were no invading tribes and no more enemies to torture words out of. All of the land was united under the Yellow Emperor, and

Cangjie went back to his family's place along the Yellow River to live quietly.

He understood the curse that people of the Yellow Emperor's tribes often placed on one another: "May you live in interesting times."

But when Cangjie sighed tonight, lying awake in bed because of some tiny noise, it was a sigh of happiness and peace, as peaceful as his heart could be after such a life. Every time he was startled awake these days, he had the privilege of reminding himself that those years were over. He'd been instrumental in helping The Yellow Emperor come into power. And by some miracle, the world had become quiet.

Cangjie looked over at his wife, who he hadn't seen for years at a time during the fighting. She breathed quick breaths with her small lungs, sleeping as deep as the night felt. He listened for his young son sleeping in the other room, his son who had been born during the fighting, who he'd barely known until these last years since returning to his village as a war hero and a man haunted by his dreams.

Every day those dreams became more distant. Every night he woke with a start became more of a comfort.

He smiled as his heart slowed to its regular rhythm.

Cangjie was living in uninteresting times.

Cangjie was bored.

And he was absolutely ecstatic about it.

He had had enough adventure for several lives already, and Cangjie was only now in the middle of his.

He sighed again, a happier sigh. He looked forward

to another day watching the people in his village bustle about with cleaning their water pots, whacking their cows with dried bamboo stalks to make them move, mending their roofs against the coming winter.

The very act of staying in one place took so much work. It was fascinating to Cangjie, after so many years of staying alive by staying in motion.

It was still dark, but Cangjie rose from his sleeping mat. He stood up slowly, making sure his wife wasn't woken up by his movement. He walked across the ground over to the door to their home and looked out into the darkness.

The home had been bestowed to Cangjie and his family when he had returned to his place as a hero of war and a close advisor to the Yellow Emperor. The thatch on the roof never leaked and the walls held out even the strongest winds. But Cangjie's favorite thing about this house was the spectacular view from out this door and across the valley. When it was light outside, Cangjie could see seven different mountain ridges, each one lighter in shade than the one before it. It heartened him to think of all of his travels as a messenger, and how his efforts had made all the lands he could see into one great tribe at peace. He sat on the step and listened to the world in the dark. He heard the Yellow River flowing down in the valley. He heard the leaves dance along their tree limbs.

And Cangjie thought that this moment, here in his doorway in the dark and looking blindly out at the seven mountain ridges, would be a wonderful way to end his story, were he to find a poet to tell it for him. If there were only a poet to keep telling his story to listeners for ages to come, Cangjie would want the poet to end it with him sitting here, when all was quiet and peaceful. He wanted his story to end with that happy feeling that a good poet can give an audience, even in the most woeful of times.

Already the poets were changing the story of the battles Cangjie had fought in and the history of the tribes coming together. They were forgetting certain things and exaggerating others. Some men were becoming gods on earth, to hear the way the poets sang about them. And it was as if other great men had never existed.

As much as he wanted to forget whole seasons of his past life, he resented the power of the poets to change the way things had happened. No story was made of stone, no words could last forever.

Cangjie sighed, because he was powerless to change that. He knew he was living in his own happy ending right at that moment, and that, were he blessed enough, he would have many more years to live in it, whether a poet ever told his story or not.

Yet Cangjie couldn't mistake the worry in his gut that something was coming to take him out of his happiness. No matter how much he wanted it to be so, his was not a life meant to be blessed with boredom.

So he waited there on the step. He was the happiest man in the world right at that moment, and at least he had that.

If the poets told his story, it would end here in his greatest happiness, but even the greatest poets wouldn't be able to explain how he felt.

The first blue hint of light was just bleeding over the horizon in the east, and Cangjie stared at it. He was happier than he'd ever felt.

And yet.

Cangjie had lived enough lifetimes already to know —like the best poets know—that stories do not end with their endings.

Cangjie knew that endings were illusions, and that it was only the magic of the poets that made life make sense.

Cangjie watched the blue light in the east brighten the slightest bit more, until he heard a stirring behind him in the hut. He smiled at the flopping noise his son's feet made on the ground, and he felt as if his heart would burst as he watched Shoyu move toward him and come out to the doorway, where he sat down beside Cangjie and looked out into the valley.

In the faint light of the morning, Shoyu looked like a young man. When Cangjie had left to fight, his wife had been pregnant, though she had not told him so. The message of his son's birth, when it arrived, almost made Cangjie steal away from all the battles and the messages he carried across the land. But to do so would have been a great dishonor, or worse. Likely it would have meant Cangjie's death. So he continued his duties and carried his messages with a greater burden.

And now that he was home again, Cangjie cherished moments like this one, sitting next to his son, neither of them speaking. This silence was a great solace. He had quickly become accustomed to his stable, quiet life when he returned from the fighting, and every day he loved it more deeply.

He liked the slow days and the uneventful nights. He liked hearing the news from distant villages from the travelers and peddlers who came along the road. It was from them that Cangjie had learned that the Yellow Emperor had defeated and brought together the tribes of the Shennong and the Juili, and now formed the great Huaxia tribe. Cangjie had known of this the moment his communications helped defeat Chi You at the Battle of Zhoulu, but it took almost three seasons before the official messengers arrived with the news.

Cangjie smiled as he thought back on the day this message had come. The villagers had hailed the messengers as heroes, had a great celebration of the peace they foresaw for many years to come.

The role of the messenger had changed. Cangjie and many others brought terrible news during war. Information about a forthcoming ambush. Orders for an assassination of a rival leader. Directions for battle that would surely result in the deaths of many men.

Even after victory, messengers reported casualties and deaths.

But now, when the world was calm, messengers were heroes when they brought news of nothing much changing.

Cangjie smiled. He'd left to fight in the Emperor's army as an idealistic young man willing to die. Indeed, he had thought he would die. And in those grueling years, he came to know many great men who did die, men much greater than he. Yet, somehow, Cangjie did not die. Somehow the swords only grazed him, the messages reached him in time, the dragons in the forest failed to find him. And Cangjie returned home a hero, to a much finer house, a life much easier than the one he'd left years earlier.

And now, here was this boy, his son. Cangjie noticed the way Shoyu's jaw was suddenly strong in profile and his face now had the sharp edges of a young man's. He was now almost grown, and that made Cangjie sad. His son sat on the step respectfully, not speaking until spoken to.

"This time of day, when the first light comes over the horizon, is a dangerous one in times of war," Cangjie said. "Son, if you choose to enter the army of the Yellow Emperor, you must remember this."

Shoyu nodded. He would remember.

"It is most dangerous because, if you are out in the field and there is light, then you are no longer invisible. This is especially dangerous for messengers."

Shoyu waited a moment, then asked, "Did men die carrying your messages?"

"Yes. Many times. Often right in this time of day, when they were suddenly caught in the light."

As he said these words, Jum sum, god of sleep and dreams, conjured moments up from Cangjie's past. He saw many times when he had escaped with his life with only a sliver of luck. Hiding in a tree. Swimming blindly across a river. Disguising himself as a farmer among a herd of yak.

But also before his eyes flashed the faces of many brave men who had died while carrying the messages in their minds. Their last thoughts were of family, friends, their villages, and the message they carried.

Their faces burned in his eyes, but Cangjie could not remember any of the messages that these brave men held in their minds when they died.

When was a life worth mere words?

Cangjie was thinking of all these men when he saw a slight movement at the edge of the woods.

Something was not right.

Instincts from the tumultuous times returned to his blood. Cangjie's heart beat a thunderous gallop.

The noises at night awoke him because of moments like this, when his past would appear in his present and peaceful life. An assassin loyal to Chi You, perhaps, or the son of a Shennong general out to avenge his father's death.

"Go inside. Now," he told Shoyu. "Go to your mother and take shelter with her. Be prepared to defend her if something should happen to me."

His son flew inside without a word. Cangjie heard his footsteps hurrying through the house to where his wife slept. He was now alone. None of the servants would be up yet, either. And he had nothing to use to defend himself.

Cangjie watched the spot where he had seen the movement. It was now the last moment before the day became full light, when the messenger must hide and wait out the sun, or disguise himself in plain sight.

The movement that Cangjie thought he saw at the edge of the woods looked like the work of a messenger hiding. But so far as Cangjie knew, there was no war. What had a messenger to fear?

He left the step and began walking towards the spot. Cangjie had lived so many years so close to death, he would be content when it came for him. But his greatest fear was that the killing would not stop with him, that the resentment would be so great that they would attack his wife and his son, perhaps even the entire village.

Cangjie knew he would have to defend himself with the one weapon he did have: his words.

He was still a great length from the nearest tree when he saw a man kneeling among the leaves and vines. The man rested his forehead on the earth and whispered loudly to himself. He seemed to be nearly crying.

From a safe distance, Cangjie called to him.

"You there!" he said. "Make yourself known."

The man turned and looked out of the woods at him. Cangjie had many times seen true terror in another man's eyes, sometimes in the moment just before his death, and sometimes just in receiving the orders that would certainly lead to it. It was that very look that he saw in the eyes of this man.

"Master Cangjie!" cried the man.

As the man made his way out of the woods, Cangjie could see there was no danger. The messenger was thin and weak. His hemp robe was dirty and in tatters, hanging limply over his shoulders. The man walked with great labor from his poor state, but also, Cangjie thought, from the burden of what he carried, though he had no pack, no food, nothing.

"My name is Shen," mumbled the man. "I have been sent by the Emperor. His Greatness summons you to his palace for..." And at this, Shen grew silent and he looked at Cangjie in terror again.

Cangjie understood. Shen carried the burden of the messenger.

"Come inside," he told Shen. "Let my servants bathe you and fetch you clean robes. May you rest your feet at our fire and eat until you are full enough for a lifetime. I was a messenger once. I know how you feel."

"Master Cangjie," Shen said, "that is why my shame is so great. I know my task is to summon you to the Emperor's palace and to accompany and protect you on our return journey. But I fear that I do not understand how to tell you *why* you have been summoned."

Cangjie's stomach turned in a fear he had not felt since the Battle of Zhoulu. He did not want to leave his family and his quiet life. He had been through enough for many lifetimes already. Already he felt a great shame, for his mind raced to create a story of why he could not possibly travel to the Emperor's palace. He imagined the pain of Xiezhi's horn goring him for his lie. He knew that he must go, in spite of all his heart's wishes not to.

Yet Cangjie put away his feelings for that moment to pursue the question.

"What do you mean, good Shen?" he asked. "What do you not understand?"

"The Emperor summons you to...to... Oh, Master Cangjie, the Emperor desires for you to take these words that we speak and, I do not understand, but... *capture* them."

Cangjie's servants treated Shen very well, giving him all the food his stomach could hold and washing weeks of grime from his skin and hair. Shen fell into a deep sleep and snored loudly, and it was only then that Cangjie could face his wife and son and tell them he had been summoned by the Emperor.

He kept a strong face while he told them, like the soldier he once was, but inside his heart was cracking in two.

"We are not at war with ourselves any longer," he said. "I am being summoned for some task by the Emperor and will return home before the new moon appears." He told them they would rejoice together this evening to celebrate their time together, and they would hold another celebration when he returned.

When Shoyu nodded solemnly and walked out of their home and into the village, Cangjie felt both terrible guilt and relief. He sighed and held his wife close to him.

"I do not wish to go on this journey," he confessed to her.

"Ah, you great men. You can never be content. That

is my fate, that what makes me love you is what keeps you away from me."

Cangjie's heart decided it would not go, though his body knew he would. He consoled himself that he would have one last night with his wife before he left.

But when Shen awoke, he was deeply embarrassed at how long he had slept and insisted they leave at once.

"The Emperor requires you with the greatest haste," he told Cangjie.

So they left soon after, carrying what provisions they could. As he went, Cangjie's wife whispered in his ear that she would miss him.

"I hope you are correct, that you will return before the new moon. I pray to Zhong Kui to keep you safe from evil spirits along your way. But dear Cangjie, I cannot help feeling that you will be gone for much longer than that. I feel that you are setting off on your greatest adventure only now, and the world will have changed when you return."

Cangjie held her tight and stayed silent, for there were no words he could find to use. For all his travels and glory in battle, his wife again proved herself wiser about the world than he could ever be.

With great sadness choking his lungs, Cangjie left.

For weeks he and Shen traveled along the roads, drinking from streams and sleeping under their hemp blankets among the trees. When they could, they relied on the hospitality of strangers in the tiny villages they came across, for food and sometimes a restful sleep.

Shen proved himself a deft hunter. He kept his bow in his hands always and was such an accurate shot that, during the many weeks of their journey, Cangjie rarely felt hungry. Shen knew many ways of starting a fire to keep them warm and to cook the bounty of his hunting. Cangjie much enjoyed the fires, and sometimes found himself staring blankly into the dancing flames for hours. It was a luxury he was never able to enjoy in all his secret traveling as a messenger.

While they traveled along on their feet, Cangjie and Shen shared stories. Cangjie told Shen about his years as a messenger and how he became the Master of Communications during the great battles alongside the Yellow Emperor. He often remarked how this journey, though it may be long, was such easy going. They traveled by daylight and rested well at night, worrying only about the dangers in Nature and not of the danger of a fellow man loyal to the other side.

They told each other old stories, legends they each knew in different ways. They told of the demon spirits and winged monkeys, of Shenlong the rain dragon, of Tam Kung, the god who could predict weather. They asked each other if, in all of their travels as messengers, they had seen any of these creatures of legend, and neither had. It was no matter. Such old stories comforted them both.

Shen then told of the developing world in the capitol around the Emperor's palace, of the travelers from strange lands bringing exotic items, and the ways that the clothing had begun to be as colorful as Nature itself, bright yellows and reds and greens, not the dirty brown of the heavy robes both of them wore. He described the method the Yellow Emperor had devised to surround the city with a tall and thick wall, to protect it from invaders. Cangjie could not conceive of how such a thing was possible, a shelf of earth standing upright like a man.

Cangjie had traveled greater distances than anyone he knew, but now he was seeing how vast this great world was. This journey of weeks was only covering a small portion of it. The farthest regions of the Huaxia, Shen said, could take a full four seasons to reach.

A world so vast did not seem possible. But Cangjie nodded and pretended to be wiser than he felt he was.

And the closer they moved toward the Palace, the more Cangjie felt he knew very little. The roads became wider, firmer, more carefully maintained. And the travelers along the road became more numerous. Men walked alongside horses loaded with dry goods, asking Cangjie and Shen if they had anything to trade. Other men asked for work or food. Cangjie saw the most ornate clothing he had ever seen as they walked along. Warm shawls from animal fur, laced with shiny rocks. Threads seemed to be used not to hold seams together but to decorate clothing. Bright head coverings not made of thatch or hemp, but of a material Cangjie had never before seen that looked as smooth as milk.

Shen seemed to grow both more excited and more nervous as they approached the palace. He was eager to be finished with their long journey—for he had been on it exactly twice as long as Cangjie had. And yet he feared going into the palace and facing the Emperor, he confessed, as they began their last day's walk from the outskirts of the Capitol in toward the palace.

When they reached the city walls, Shen stood still as if he could travel no step further.

He said, "I am afraid, Master Cangjie, that I was supposed to illuminate you as to the task the Emperor's is asking of you, though I still do not understand what that is."

"Dear Shen," Cangjie said. "Do not worry. You have done very well in your duty. You are a masterful hunter and a great companion. I have known the Emperor for many years—we were together during the great battles with the Shennong and Jiuli. I will make sure he understands how well you have honored him in bringing me here."

Shen bowed and smiled. Yet he could not muster the strength to say much more as they were allowed through the gates and into the city, where the roads were laden with stone rather than dirt and the houses were finer and stronger than any of the village huts they had seen along their journey.

As they approached the palace, servants came rushing out to meet them. They brought Cangjie and Shen new blankets to wrap about them as cloaks, and Cangjie had never before felt material of such softness. They brought them gourds of water to drink and Cangjie had never tasted such cool water outside of winter. They ushered Cangjie away to one end of the palace so fast that he only had time to shout a quick farewell to Shen, promising they would talk again soon.

Cangjie was taken to a room like none he had ever seen before. The floors were of stone as smooth as a frozen puddle. The place he was to sleep was not the usual mat he was accustomed to back in his village. This was a bed ten times the size of that one, a puffy blob filled with thousands of tiny feathers. There was a bowl large enough for a man to sit in, and that is what the servants had Cangjie do, filling it with warm water and pouring it over his dirty, road-weary skin.

The servants doused his hair and scrubbed his head to remove the grime and debris. Then, they massaged fragrant oils into his hair and skin, things Cangjie had never smelled before in his life. The smells were related to things in Nature, but were powerful, aggressive to his nose. He could not find a way to escape them as he breathed, so heavily they coated his hair.

When he got out of his bath, the servants rubbed him gently with soft cloths and then fanned his naked body with large dried fronds. Cangjie was terribly embarrassed, but also found it so ridiculous that he struggled to keep his laughter silent.

Finally, they put a heavy, soft robe around Cangjie and left him alone. He was to sleep, they told him, for the Emperor wanted him rested before they were to meet. When they left, Cangjie dropped the robe off his shoulders as quickly as he could. He lay his naked body back on the gigantic bed and felt it compress and almost swallow him in its softness.

It felt like the bed might suffocate him, but Cangjie drifted off into a deep and restful sleep, his last one for many, many nights.

Cangjie opened his eyes in terror. Where was he? What was engulfing him in softness? But as his eyes adjusted to the light streaming into the palace room and he felt his legs and feet aching beneath the blanket, he remembered and lay back again to rest a bit longer.

It was then that he turned to his side, blinked, and saw two eyes staring back at him.

Cangjie screamed, scrambled backwards out of the bed, found himself standing naked and looking frantically for some sort of thing he could use as a weapon, when he heard hysterical laughing.

He looked again and recognized his old friend, who was also his Emperor.

"Your Highness," Cangjie said, and bowed. He stayed bent over to hide his body.

The Emperor came walking around the bed carrying the robe that Cangjie had discarded on the floor, and put it around Cangjie's shoulders. When he had wrapped himself and tied the sash, Cangjie stood up and looked at the Emperor in the eyes. There was that smile again.

"Master Cangjie," he said. He patted Cangjie on the

back. "Come, old friend, you must be famished."

They ate a great feast for such an early hour, with servants rushing back and forth bringing what seemed an unlimited supply of the cool, clean water, along with exotic fruits, and wine. Before him on a platter was a leg of goat that had been cooked over a fire. It was covered in the strangest spices that tasted to Cangjie like the earth in faraway landscapes, and the bark of exotic trees in warmer climates, and the heat of the sun against his tongue.

The Yellow Emperor was happy to see Cangjie. While they ate he asked how these last years had been for him, and whether he was satisfied with his living arrangements and his life in his village, and how many wives Cangjie had, how many children. Cangjie answered, but did not say how uncomfortable he felt with his servants always around. He only expressed his thankfulness, and how gracious the Emperor was.

When they had finished eating, the Emperor sent all the servants away and it was just the two of them at the table.

"Cangji*eeeeeeee*," the Emperor growled in his friendly way. "Come, now, we are alone. We have been through so much together. Tell me, without lies, how you are."

"Your Highness, I am very happy in my quiet life at home."

"Yet a quiet life means a small life, dear friend."

Cangjie said nothing, even though he disagreed.

The Emperor said, "Master Cangjie, you and I, I'm afraid, were not made for quiet lives. It is not an honor to be bestowed on us. Dear friend, it is too late and we have been through too much, and we must carry with us the burden of living great lives. Come with me."

He stood and Cangjie followed him out of the dining hall and into a great passageway, so tall it seemed a mountain could fit beneath its ceiling. Cangjie's entire village could have fit inside the passageway.

"While you were enjoying your quiet life, good friend, I was traveling across my territories and visited the East. There I saw the beast Bai Ze," said the Yellow Emperor, his voice echoing down from the great high ceiling.

"Your Highness!" Cangjie said.

"Indeed, old friend. He had nine eyes and six horns and the face of a man, and I learned much from him, more than any man can understand about this world and the spirits in it. After this, I cannot see the world the same as it was. I must act on what I now know."

The Yellow Emperor bent close to Cangjie's face and looked sharply into his eyes. "I trust good Shen has told you why I summoned you?" the Emperor said as they began to walk down the corridor.

"Yes, your Highness, but...I'm ashamed to say I did not understand what he meant."

"Ah, I did not expect Shen would be able to grasp what it is I want you to do. Few men can. Nevertheless, he will be richly rewarded for delivering you here safely to me."

Cangjie felt his face flush in anger—he was very capable of journeying safely on his own. He was a messenger and had faced great danger many times. Though perhaps the Emperor had forgotten that.

The Emperor turned and led him down a long wing of the palace where the ceiling was lower and the doors grew less extravagant.

"The allure of a quiet life is great," the Emperor said. "It is as seductive as the most beautiful woman. But Master Cangjie, you must understand. We have the blood of many men on our hands. Not only the blood of our enemies in the uprising, but of our comrades who died alongside us. And now we have won, so we have the lives of everyone across the land in our hands now, as well."

The Emperor was walking very fast and Cangjie, on his sore feet, had to run painfully to keep up. They stopped before a plain wooden door.

"I beg your forgiveness, your Highness, but I do not seek out such responsibility," Cangjie said.

"Ah, dear Cangjie. That is the greatest kind of greatness, indeed," the Emperor said with a flourish as he opened the door.

Inside were about a dozen men sitting at long tables. They had strands of hemp rope before them and were tying them in various kinds of knots in a series along the rope. Cangjie recognized what they were doing at once. These men were the official recordkeepers of the kingdom.

All of the recordkeepers looked up, startled by the loud bang of the door opening, and stared at Cangjie and the Yellow Emperor. One of them suddenly stood and bowed, and then all the others did, and they stayed there, crouched, while the Emperor looked out into the room. There were ropes in piles, hanging from rafters, and draped in many loops around the recordkeepers' necks. Each rope had an intricate series of knots along its length.

"Cangjie, what are these good men? They are responsible for recording everything. And what is this, indeed?" The Emperor picked up the length of rope nearest to him on the table and held it dangling from his fingers.

"Your Highness, I do not know," Cangjie said.

"It is rope!" the Emperor laughed. "And what is this?" He pointed to the last knot in its length.

"I do not know, your Highness."

"You know, without knowing you know," said the Emperor.

"It is a knot," Cangjie said. Then he added, "Your Highness."

The Emperor's face lit in delight. "Ah, great Cangjie! You see the problem! That knot could signify that a farmer owes his neighbor a chicken, or how Chi You was defeated by you and me and our comrades. One is a quiet life, one is not. Yet both are represented with a knot like this one, and only these good men can tell us which is which."

The Emperor tossed the rope back on the table and left the room. Cangjie and the recordkeepers stood there staring at each other in disbelief and confusion. Finally, Cangjie came back to his mind and followed the Emperor out into the hallway in time to see him stepping out an opening into a courtyard garden. Cangjie met him there, sitting on a stone bench surrounded by the most meticulous arrangement of natural beauty he had ever seen.

"Master Cangjie, as much as I honor the toil of those men, we must do better. We must find a way to make our words and deeds last longer than the mere moments we take to speak and do them."

"Your Highness," asked Cangjie carefully, "do our artists not do a fine job capturing our past deeds?"

"Yes, yes, indeed, yes. But it is not enough for one vase or one wall or one tapestry to tell the story of what happened. There are too many words that are not in these works of art. And there is not enough of the art. It is not right that the Emperor should have all the pieces of artwork that tell this story. For, I do not presume there are fine works of art everywhere in your village?"

"No, your Highness."

"And why shouldn't there be? Do your beloved neighbors not deserve to hear the stories of our deeds? Do they not deserve the ability to tell stories of their own and pass them along to others who also cannot afford the luxury of the fine artwork?"

"Your Highness, I..." Cangjie said, but trailed off. He couldn't wrap his mind around this concept. He'd never thought that a lowly villager would have a story to tell that needed to be told twice. A story told many times would become a legend that everyone would simply tell their children, with words they speak aloud. But the Emperor was seeking something more, something permanent.

Cangjie said, "Your Highness, they could use the rope and knots, could they not?"

The Emperor laughed hard. "My dear comrade! If we continue using ropes and knots for everything we must record, we will cover our entire land in the greatest spiderweb and entangle ourselves so that we can achieve nothing!"

The Emperor stood and looked around the garden.

"For you see, Great Cangjie, Master of Communication, we are living in a time of peace. But a time of peace is not a time for standing still.

"Do you not see, old friend, that when we united the tribes all across the land, that we were creating the world all over again, like the gods? That we have a chance now to make things as they should be? I have had enough of battles, and the people of this land have had enough of the lives they had before. We must make things different. Better."

He was looking out across the garden, but not looking at it. He was seeing something grand, an idea that Cangjie just did not get no matter where he looked.

"Your Highness, I humbly beg your forgiveness, but what is it you ask of me?" Cangjie finally had the courage to ask.

"To find a better method of keeping our words and deeds and stories sacred. These words and sounds that come from my mouth, and your mouth, and the mouth of the poorest farmer. I want a way for them to be recorded so that everyone can understand, yet record them as uniquely as each person who speaks the words is unique. Not a simple knot on a simple rope. Something better."

"And, dear Leader, what is this better way?" Cangjie asked.

The Emperor turned to him and smiled.

"I do not know the way. I only know that there *is* one. I am wise enough to rely on men smarter than me to find them. You begin tomorrow," said the Emperor. Cangjie stayed sitting on the stone bench and listened as the feet of the Emperor walked away slowly over the gravel path.

Cangjie looked at the garden, with its delicate bending paths and its perfect rows of greenery and its groups of red flowers together, and yellow flowers, and white flowers. It was incredibly beautiful. But was also completely unnatural. The garden was wild nature that had been tamed.

All the stories Cangjie had heard as a child, and all the stories anyone across the land had ever told, and all the words he had said to friends and comrades and his wife and travelers, these were all natural, too. And sometimes stories could be captured in an artist's painting, or signified by a knot along a length of rope, but it was natural that the words themselves were gone forever after they were spoken.

Cangjie was being asked to do an unnatural thing, to

tame nature again by capturing forever the lost words of everyone. He feared that he was being given an impossible task. He felt there was no way it could be done and be as beautiful as this very garden was.

And Cangjie sat on the bench in the middle of all that beauty and cried.

An Impossible Task

For weeks, Cangjie had everything he could ever want. He slept exactly when his body wanted to, even if it was midday. He ate the finest meats from the palace hunters and the freshest forage from the forest, because there was nothing besides the best things to eat in the palace. He had water nearby and clean robes, and his servants were always following him around to tend to his every slight need, and many needs he didn't have. They asked him many times each day if he would like a bath.

The Emperor had provided Cangjie with a luxurious room to contemplate his task. There was a grand table with heavy, ornate chairs. But there were also large, soft mats stuffed with feathers. On the walls were fantastic works of art from artists who drew and painted and wove tapestries, all depicting great events throughout the history of the land. The artwork also told stories of how the people had come to this land, showing gods, dragons, legends. Cangjie was fond of an enormous rock slab that an artist had chiseled into a shape depicting Kua Fu reaching yet again skyward to capture the sun. The Emperor had been sure to have art from each of the tribes that were now unified under his rule. Every so often, workmen responsible for the building upkeep would come in and hang a new work that depicted an event in the great battles, or showed the Emperor in some benevolent and godlike way, uniting the land, bringing peace.

It would have been a life of perfect happiness for many men.

Yet Cangjie enjoyed none of the things the Emperor provided. His life was too easy. This was the Emperor's intention, so Cangjie could use all his energy for thinking of a better way than tying knots to record words, thoughts, feelings.

In his pristine and luxurious cage of a room, Cangjie brooded for untold hours about words and the futility of capturing them. He stared out the windows of his study at the garden, thinking that his task from the Emperor was the same one given to those gardeners: to take things meant to bloom and die, but keep them seemingly in bloom forever.

But the gardeners had an advantage. A flower was a real thing that grew in real dirt. The gardeners got to hold their work in their hands, dig into the earth, and place it there to see it.

How does someone capture something to keep it alive and in bloom when there is nothing to capture? A word is just a momentary noise, Cangjie thought. Even the great giant could not capture the sun. How could a man record the air?

For many hours of each day, Cangjie brooded about

the impossible task before him, which kept him from his perfectly happy, quiet life. As Cangjie sat in his cushioned chair and despaired, he often thought of his wife back in his village. He thought about what she was doing right at the same moment—taking the bone out of the tight bun of her hair, her hair falling down her back in that beautiful waterfall. Or listening to the rain on the tightly woven roof and watching it cascade over the edge at the step, or sitting down to eat with Shoyu at the table with some roasted meat bought from a local hunter after Shoyu came home empty handed from his hunt, since Cangjie was not there to teach him.

Words, again. Did she even know Cangjie was alive? The Emperor had sent a message of their safe arrival and of the great task before Cangjie, but had the message survived the journey? Did she understand it? Was there no word she wanted to send back to him?

Certainly there was something she wished to say, but words do not work that way. Words expire, like the breath we use to make them. Cangjie kept coming back to this certainty. He had been given an impossible task.

One day he looked out the window yet again at the garden, marveling at the suddenly new red and white blooms that were not there the day before. And just then, the Emperor burst in through the doors with his usual following of servants and caretakers and assistants. Cangjie's own servants, who had grown used to an idle life since he gave them so little to do, fell off their own feathery mats onto the floor in their haste to stand, and bowed as they scrambled to their feet.

Cangjie felt his stomach knot together, his heart being strangled inside his chest.

"Your Highness," he said as he bowed.

"Master Cangjie," said the Emperor as he bowed in return. This small gesture made Cangjie feel much happier. "What new thoughts and systems have you devised with your ingenious mind these few weeks? Are the words captured, as I commanded?"

Cangjie could only stand there with his head bowed. The Emperor went on after a short silence.

"You see, I have much I need to say! There is much I must communicate to this vast land, for we are in a great new time. Yet there is only one of me!" The Emperor laughed.

"Yes, Your Highness," Cangjie said, bowing his head a little further.

"Dear Cangjie, old friend, have you any ideas?"

"No, Your Highness," said Cangjie. He thought one of the guards was about to draw his sword and slice his head off for his failure. Instead, the Emperor came forward, bending down to where Cangjie's head had sunk.

"But, good man, think of the poor recordkeepers! They are being smothered in their own mountain of knots! Ha ha!" The Emperor laughed, and many of his entourage laughed, too. Then, the Emperor motioned to the grand table, and he and Cangjie went and sat in the heavy chairs there.

"Tell me of your thoughts on your task," said the Emperor.

Cangjie told him that words are meant to bloom and die, like breath. That words and messages are so temporary that they often fail. That he had no way to even know if his own family was well, or even alive, because words are so small they can only travel the shortest of distances.

Cangjie said so many things that he did not even realize everything he said. He found himself having talked much too long, and then looked up into the Emperor's understanding eyes for a long moment of silence.

Finally the Emperor spoke.

"Ah," he said. "I see." He stood up and went over to the window. "Cangjie, I have done you no favors by putting you in this room, where I thought you would have every comfort. I have done you no good to feed you so much that you grow fat, and bathe you until you have no scent upon you. Your feet have gotten soft, haven't they?"

The Yellow Emperor stood and took Cangjie by the shoulder.

"My dear old friend, I beg your forgiveness.," the Emperor said. "I failed to remember that you are a messenger at heart. You think best out in the wild, on your feet, using your wisdom and your wits. You prefer dodging dragons and eating the fruits and seeds of the forest. Here in all this ease you are trapped. Your mind has no freedom to maneuver. The task seems impossible because it likely is impossible for you to think here."

He turned to his assistants who stood at the door silently.

"Arrange a traveling party for dawn," he told them. One of the men scurried out from the room and the Emperor turned to Cangjie.

"Tomorrow we shall leave the confines of the palace and go out into the land, together. Out there is where you shall find the answer to your task." He smiled and took a few steps toward his assistants and guards, then looked back over his shoulder. "This is so, *isn't it,* Master Cangjie?" asked the Emperor.

Cangjie, hearing the slightest thread of malice in the Emperor's question, bowed low. "Yes, Your Highness. Undoubtedly so."

The Yellow Emperor smiled.

The traveling party that was to leave at dawn did not make its way from the palace doors until afternoon. All through the night before they were to leave, Cangjie lay awake in his cloud-like bed, excited to get into the outside world, which made the next day's waiting almost unbearable.

Yet nobody else seemed to mind. There were many horses to outfit with supplies and gear, and there were many supplies—great clay urns of water, sacks of dried meat and roots, a series of grand tents and beds and furniture for the Yellow Emperor and all of the other members of the royal party. It seemed they would not want for anything while outside the palace walls.

They also would not be traveling inconspicuously. Each horse, even the lowliest one, was brushed and adorned with decorative woven blankets that had no holes anywhere on them. Cangjie, who had been wearing the luxurious animal furs given to him in the palace, felt plain and drab compared to the detailing and adornments in the horse blankets.

For each person in the traveling party, there seemed to be two members of the palace guard, armed with bows and spears, surrounding them in a perimeter just like the palace walls to defend against any ambush or horned creature. Inside the guard's circle, shamans walked among them chanting softly to ward off the mountain spirits and demons tracking them. Cangjie imagined that there would be the most peaceful sleep ever had by a traveler out in nature, should they have to sleep out in the open at any point.

And when they finally left the palace, Cangjie understood that they would not be traveling quickly. In all his years and all his journeys as a messenger, he was accustomed to taking the shortest route possible, traveling light, living by his instincts and cunning. This traveling party would do none of these. Everything was provided for, and the Emperor moved at a slow walking pace even though he was sitting atop a perfect white horse.

The Yellow Emperor had insisted on riding his own horse on this journey. Chi You had been carried in a great throne atop long planks, high in the air and shouldered by muscular, threatening men. The Yellow Emperor wanted no part of such displays of royalty. He wanted to appear as a common man.

And as they left the gates of the capitol city walls, Cangjie felt great sadness as the party turned in its slow, yawning procession to the south, away from the direction he and Shen had come by. He was surprised at his sadness, for Cangjie had not realized how much he had hoped they would travel back toward his village, that he could go home and see his wife and

Shoyu. Cangjie remembered the smell of his wife's skin, the way she was so coyly wise. He remembered her voice saying *You are setting off on your greatest adventure only now.*

Though he had been offered a fine horse to ride, Cangjie preferred to walk. He missed the feeling of the earth beneath his feet, as he had walked only on the ice-smooth rock floors of the palace for so long. At first his feet complained, but quickly they felt comfortable again, like a kind of home.

Several hours into the journey, Cangjie felt a tap on his shoulder and someone else on foot catch up to his side.

"Good Shen!" Cangjie said. He felt a rush of happiness like he had not felt since he arrived at the palace.

"Master Cangjie! Highest blessings upon you! I must speak quickly, as the guards do not want palace servants talking with the elite."

"Elite? I am no such thing! Shen, you must stay and talk with me! For, at this pace, I may well fall asleep on my very feet," Cangjie laughed.

"Yes, Master Cangjie," Shen smiled, "but I am afraid it is not allowed. I only wanted to say that our journey together was a great one in the eyes of the Emperor. I have been handsomely rewarded since our return—I have been given messenger duty within the city walls! I get to sleep in my own bed each night. And this is all the better because the Emperor has given me a wife as thanks for bringing you safely!"

Cangjie congratulated Shen while he felt a terrible lightning strike inside himself. Shen got to see his wife each evening while Cangjie was lashed to an impossible task that he must complete before he sees his own. The thought of living without his wife made it almost impossible to smile. But smile Cangjie did.

"And, Master Cangjie, my wife is with child! We will be parents soon!" Shen said. Again, Cangjie congratulated Shen, but Shen stopped him shortly. "I must ask, Master Cangjie, how you are doing with your quest to capture the words? For I want my child to know the great story of our journey. I will tell it to him many times, but I want to make sure the story is trapped for him and his children and his children's children, for all time. Have you captured the words for the Emperor yet?"

Cangjie smiled.

"I am very close to capturing the words," Cangjie kidded. "I have devised a great net, as used for fishing. Yet this special net, when spoken into, magically fills with the words from the air." He smiled at Shen, thinking Shen would laugh at his joke.

But Shen's eyes were as wide as the full moon. "Master Cangjie! This is most wonderful. I shall fill the net with the words of our journey many times when we return to the palace. Thank you, Great Communicator!"

And with that, Cangjie's friend blended back in with the servants and carriers moving in the unguarded pack at the back of the party.

During the next week of slow travel, the Emperor and his royal party each night found a house near the road as the sun moved low in the sky. Each time, the family inside would be ushered out as they bowed and gaped in shock. All of their belongings were carried out by the Yellow Emperor's guard and thrown in a large heap, and the Yellow Emperor's luxurious bed and bedroom furniture were moved in. Then the Emperor and his highest assistants and a great number of women from the palace went inside. None of the women was yet the Emperor's wife, and yet each night well beyond the darkness, the great hoots and yelps of a decadent party could be heard easily outside the walls of the humble home.

The rest of the party formed a palatial camp, with a walled perimeter patrolled by guardsmen, a great fire for cooking meat, a large trough with gourds for drinking cold water, and a vat for important travelers such as himself to stand in while servants gave baths, pouring water and rubbing with soft cloths.

Cangjie did not take a bath. He begrudgingly ate the deliciously-spiced meat, only to keep his strength up.

Never before had the outside world, wide open and dangerous, natural and beautiful, been so confining. Cangjie felt just as stifled as he had inside the thick stone walls of the palace. He had nothing to do. His pack was carried by a horse, his meals were hunted and cooked for him. His safety from earthly and supernatural threats was ensured.

In this state, Cangjie despaired. All the day long, and well into the night before the camp quieted into sleep, Cangjie listened to the words he heard. Words flew around him like mosquitoes, stinging him. They multiplied each day, growing greater and heavier like a sack full of stones upon his back. He listened to all the words he heard, and knew that these were but a tiny drop of all the words in the world. And he knew that there was no way to catch them all, as there was no way to catch all the fish in the sea or the birds in the air.

Yet fish and birds were real. A man could catch at least a few of them, and hold them in his hands. No man can catch a word, no matter how hard he tries.

So each day as they traveled, Cangjie walked in wretchedness at his impossible task.

While the party moved, the Emperor often stopped at small villages and houses along the road to speak to the citizens of the newly unified land. Many of them were astonished to see an Emperor on a horse, walking along the same roads that they used every day. The citizens bowed and said nothing in their shock. They offered what they could of water, wine, or eggs. They slaughtered goats and pigs, forced squawking chickens upon the guardsmen. The Emperor always graciously accepted, for to not do so would be a great insult.

One day, the party stopped in this manner at a small house along the road. Surrounding the house were strange trees that had been planted there many years ago, trees unlike anything that grew in the capitol. When the party came to its slow stop on the road outside of the house, a young woman emerged from the door wearing the most beautiful robe Cangjie had ever seen. It flowed like water over her and moved as freely as the wind. She was quite beautiful and reminded Cangjie of his wife.

"Greetings! I am your Emperor," called the Yellow Emperor to her.

"You are not the Yellow Emperor," the woman said. "You are much too young to be an Emperor."

The traveling party all laughed while Cangjie felt a rush of fear for the woman's life. Yet the Yellow Emperor smiled.

"You see the great party I am with, do you not? Surely you must see that the Emperor is here before you, with all of these supplies and men?"

"Yes, it would seem. Yet surely, whoever is the Yellow Emperor is also a man himself? And were he to not travel with such a group, he would seem only a man like any other, would he not?"

Cangjie thought one of the guardsmen would take his bow and shoot her through the neck for her insult any second now, but instead, the Yellow Emperor got down off of his horse with an intrigued glimmer in his eyes. He walked up close to the woman.

"Tell me," he said, bowing low before her, "where did you get this material for your robe?" He reached out and felt it between his fingers. Then, like he couldn't believe it, he felt it with his whole hand, then the back of his fingers, down along her arm and back up toward her hand.

"Here," the woman said and gestured at her home.

"This is not traded from a nearby port, from some exotic land?" asked the Emperor.

"There is no nearby port, as an Emperor should know," she said. "This robe was made from the worms that inhabit these trees my ancestors planted."

"You mean to say that you made this fine material?" asked the Emperor.

"Is the great Yellow Emperor impressed?" she asked with a smile.

"You must show me these worms and how you have made this robe," the Emperor said. A few of his close assistants walked with them, as well as a few guards. Cangjie watched as the woman led the Emperor through the trees and plucked these tiny worms off of them and unwound the cocoon surrounding them. The beautiful woman took the Emperor into the house for a long while.

After the sun had moved nearly halfway across the sky, one of the assistants came out to the party and walked up to Cangjie. The Emperor had sent for him.

"Ah, Master Cangjie," said the Emperor when he arrived. He was sitting at a crude table with the woman, with tiny threads unspooling all across it. "This is the worm from the trees outside here," he said, holding up a tiny speck that Cangjie could barely see. "Leizu tells me this is a silkworm, from the silkworm tree. Which means that this," he said, motioning to the fine threads all over the table, "is silk."

The Emperor waved one of his assistants over to Cangjie and asked him to stand up. The assistant took away Cangjie's rough robe and draped one made of this silk across his back. It felt like warm liquid on his skin, yet it was dry. It was like eating the fattiest morsel of meat, like his own body could not get enough of it even as it was touching it everywhere it could. Cangjie felt warm and protected, yet as comfortable as if he were naked.

"Great Cangjie, you have traveled over many parts of this land as a messenger, have you not?" asked the Emperor.

"Yes, Your Highness."

"And what have you seen of the clothing of the people of this land?"

"I'm sorry, Your Highness? The people's robes? They are as they always are. As they always have been."

"They are full of holes, then?" asked the Yellow Emperor. "They rub roughly against the people's skin and then tear easily after they age? They must be mended constantly? They do only a poor job at best of keeping the cold winds out?"

Cangjie had never thought in such a way as this about the rough hemp blankets and robes he had always worn. The clothing had kept him alive for his whole life and he had never expected more of it.

"Yes, Your Highness," he said. "It is as you say with the robes of the people."

"We must then cultivate these silkworm trees to make more silk. The people of the land need better clothing than we have always had," the Emperor said. The beautiful woman smiled.

"But, Your Highness," said Cangjie, "surely such a fine material should be reserved for the Emperor?"

"Dear Cangjie," the Yellow Emperor said. "The Emperor is only a man like any other, is he not?" He looked over at the woman again. Then he stood up and told the group that they would go outside now, for he had an announcement to make.

On the way out the door, the Emperor took Cangjie by his silken sleeve and pulled him in close.

"You see how Leizu has done, do you not? There is a better way, a natural way, to improve this new world we have made. We must only be wise enough to see what is already all around us," he said, nodding at Cangjie.

And as they assembled outside, the Emperor quieted the traveling party. He announced that these trees were to be bred and grown in all parts of the land, so that everyone could have robes as fine as this. He assigned members of the party to begin the cultivation process of the silkworm trees and others to begin sending them to the distant regions.

Then he quieted the crowd again. He announced

that, due to her wisdom in improving the lives of all people in the land, he would take Leizu as his wife. The traveling party would return to the palace in the morning and begin preparations for the royal wedding.

An uproar of joyous noise came from the traveling party, and there began a great feast so quickly that, to Cangjie, it seemed like magic.

For the whole day and late into the night, it was as joyous a time as Cangjie had ever seen. He enjoyed wearing the silk robe around the feast and having others put it on. And late in the evening, he made sure to find Shen to try on the great robe, and then sneak away before Shen could return it to him.

But as he lay in his tent on his soft bed, Cangjie felt like he shared none of the joy that he heard still going on around him in the dark. He longed to see his wife and tell her of his troubled mind. He wished for her consoling touch and the wise words she would say.

And yet his task—to find a way to catch the words—was the very thing that was keeping him from seeing her and hearing her words.

Leizu had succeeded without even trying. Cangjie did not feel his task was possible to achieve that way. He felt that the very words he was to somehow capture were too valuable, to precious, to important to life to ever be caught.

Early the next morning, just as the sun was making the horizon the slightest blue, Cangjie arose from his comfortable camp bed. There were still some revelers who stirred among the traveling party, though most had gone to bed or fallen unexpectedly into sleep against tent walls or in shrubs sometime in the middle of the darkness.

Cangjie packed only what basic necessities he imagined he would need. His hemp robe, a knife, a bow. He was tempted by the many silk robes that were worn by the sleeping people he saw all around him, and could've easily taken one of the ones draped in among a tree's branches or across a horse's back, or puddled at the feet of naked legs protruding out from under a blanket. But he did not want to succumb to the new clothing so quickly.

He spotted the bright robe he had been given earlier, still draped over the shoulders of Shen.

"Good Shen," he whispered. Shen stirred, then jumped. It was that dangerous time of day. A messenger never forgets. "It is only me, Cangjie."

"Master Cangjie," said Shen drunkenly, relaxing

back into his bed.

"Shen, you must give the Emperor a message for me. I am not accompanying the party back to the palace. I am off to complete my task and capture words. I hope to be back at the palace in time for the wedding festivities. Will you give the Emperor this message?"

Shen nodded and grunted. So Cangjie left, though he did not know if his words would reach the Yellow Emperor or not. That was the way with words.

For many days, Cangjie traveled alone. He often did not travel along the roads, but went across the wilds from village to village in the shortest distance he could. He slept in the open air, listened closely for demon spirits he knew were there yet had never seen. In between the infrequent occasions he was able to kill a rodent or take down a bird with his bow so that he had meat to eat, he foraged in the woods for tubers and roots and mushrooms.

When he was alone in nature, Cangjie used no words. He walked for hours thinking about what the Yellow Emperor was asking of him.

It occurred to him that none of the animals and none of the plants of the world had use for words, either. Animals had calls like words, but they were so few and so simple. None of the creatures of the earth had any desire to capture their noises and communications. They had no need to.

And neither did humans, Cangjie thought. The only human who thought this task was of use was the Yellow Emperor. And did he not admit that he was also just a man? Who was he alone to see a need for something in the world?

Yet Cangjie knew he must succeed, or he would die without ever sharing words again with his wife and his son.

So at each village Cangjie encountered, he returned to his words. He asked to speak with the wisest and the eldest members of the community. And at each village, Cangjie's wonder grew at the size of the task before him, and at the changes he saw across the land.

One night, a powerful thunderstorm came upon Cangjie so suddenly that even Tam Kung could not have forseen it. By a stroke of luck he found a rock outcropping to hide within while he watched the lightning across the night sky. In the morning, Cangjie made his way into a village to find all the citizens marveling at a roof that stood still and tight as an animal's skin atop its house while all the other thatch roofs were mangled or completely gone.

"It is a strange frond, woven together with a new method taught to us by messengers from the palace," the eldest man told him. "This was our first roof to make in this manner, and now we have the good fortune of making them all like this."

In another village, Cangjie was invited into the home of the wisest and the eldest man, who gave him warm goat milk, and asked Cangjie question after question about his journey and his time in the palace and the wishes of the Emperor. Cangjie spoke on and on without realizing he was doing so, until he remembered that he had come into Master Zhang's home in search of his wisdom.

"Master Zhang, your neighbors consider you the wisest in the village, yet you have spoken little today."

"Yes," said Zhang. And he sat still and smiling, and said nothing more.

"Why have you not told me the wise things you must know?" asked Cangjie.

"One does not become wise by speaking," Zhang said.

Many hours later, after Cangjie had said many more words that would be lost forever to a man less wise than Zhang, he finally explained his task of capturing the words. He asked Master Zhang how this could be done.

"It cannot."

"I see," said Cangjie, slumping down in his chair.

"This is as it should be. For the gods have given only man the ability to make the sound of a word. Yet they give us no way to capture a sound, and instead make words as ungraspable as the air, you see?" Zhang looked around him for a moment. "Is there a way for a word to make no sound?"

"No, Master Zhang," said Cangjie.

"You see? What are words for? To learn. And how can one learn from a word with no sound?"

When he left early in the morning, as the elder Master Zhang was still asleep, Cangjie was thinking still about the mystery of a word with no sound. As he entered into the woods and left behind the world of words, such an impossible idea seemed equal to finally seeing a mountain spirit. In time the thought faded, like a voice and a word.

Many days later, Cangjie came to a village along a bend in a wide river. He was surprised to find a fisherman on the bank wearing a silk robe in a blue color much like that of the water in front of him. He asked where he had gotten the robe.

"From a boat that floated up from the Emperor's palace. We traded a week's worth of fish for them. Always there are more fish to catch, but robes like this we'll never see again."

"It is the Emperor's idea that everyone across the land have such a robe, I understand."

The fisherman grunted. Cangjie asked to speak to the wisest and the eldest men in the village.

"There are none here," he said. "We are a poor village. We have this river. The wisest leave by it because they are wise. The eldest get swept away by it as soon as they are too old to master it any longer."

"Is there anyone skilled in speech and words?" Cangjie asked.

"No. Fish have no use for those." The fisherman cast his net out into the river again. "There is a man who arrived here by boat from elsewhere, though. Leaving soon, I imagine."

Cangjie asked who this man was.

"Calls himself a poet. I don't have much use for him," the fisherman said.

Cangjie made his way into town and found the poet,

outside the earthen structure where fish dried, reciting lines for several confused onlookers. A great thrill ran up the skin on Cangjie's back, for he recognized the voice at once.

Cangjie hurried up to join the small group of listeners. As soon as he did, the great poet Wei broke his line.

"Cangjie, The Great Communicator," Wei said with a smile.

"Wei, Master Poet," Cangjie smiled back.

"Friends, it is there the story ends," Wei said to the villagers. He held out his hands for donations—food, stones, trinkets—but none of the villagers had anything to give him and they turned and walked away. Wei shrugged and turned to his old friend, Cangjie.

"It has been many years," he said, taking Cangjie's arm and leading him toward the river. Along the way to the beautiful bluff that Wei took them to, where the river shimmered below them as if they had been struck in the head with a hard blow, the two reminisced about their short but vibrant time together in the Yellow Emperor's army, in the early days before the great battles with the Shennong and the Jiuli.

Back then, Wei was already a well-known poet who traveled the land telling the history of times to anyone who would listen—and would pay him. In the poems he recited, Wei spun tales of the evil invading tribes and the wondrous time to be when the land was united under the Yellow Emperor. These tales were completely fictional on both accounts, which Wei conjured up differently and spontaneously each time, for his own entertainment. He also collected information on the neighboring tribes, as a kind of traveling spy.

Cangjie, as Master of Communications and messengers, met up with Wei occasionally to take Wei's information from the land and report it to the leaders in the Yellow Emperor's army. At meetings with much wine, Wei regaled Cangjie with his tales of evil and benevolence, the fantastical fictions the poet rattled off, sending them both into deep laughing well into the darkness.

And here in this poor fishing village, retelling each other these old stories, the two men again laughed deeply and loudly. They told each other of their lives since the Yellow Emperor came to rule the unified tribes. Wei had continued on as a traveling poet, telling the history of the land, though now with all of the recent changes, he was informing people of their new benevolent Emperor and the greatness of the times they lived in.

After many hours of talk, filled with laughter so hard the men's eyes watered, and sadness at the losses each recollected, and the ways their youth had passed them by like a forgotten conversation, Cangjie sighed and asked his old friend the poet to sit down.

"Master Poet, I am traveling now on a mission for the Yellow Emperor."

"Oh? And what is his Highness too lazy to seek out for himself that he has sent you to do for him?" joked

Wei.

"He wants me to find a way to capture words. To make the sounds of communication permanent and forever, rather than recording only through artwork and knots in ropes."

For many minutes, Wei sat silently, thinking. He was a man who lived by his words, and this was an earthquake of an idea for the poet.

Finally he spoke, but it was not in a poetic way.

"What is there to make record of, that a knot in a rope will not suffice?" Wei asked. He looked out at the river and watched it pass down below them.

Wei said, "We are not at war any longer. We are in such peace as to have no events at all. My poems of these days are about the wonderful comfort of a new kind of robe. This is not the topic of great poetry."

Cangjie laughed and Wei smiled at him. Then he spoke again.

"My friend. My old, dear friend. What is the use of such a thing as a captured word, in place for all time? Is a word imprisoned any different than a man imprisoned?"

He looked out at the river again and was quiet for a long time as he thought. Finally, Wei spoke again.

"Who am I, to need to say more than my time and my breath will allow? Who is the Yellow Emperor to think differently than this?"

Cangjie did not know what words to use in answer. There was nothing to say.

Cangjie and Wei made their way back toward the capitol city over the next few days. As they went, many travelers joined them along the roads, for the word was that this wedding celebration was to be the largest, most decadent event in anyone's life, such was the love the Yellow Emperor had for his bride.

"Everyone wishes to live in important times," Wei said. "And each time must find importance wherever it can. Apparently, a wedding will do."

Everyone in the capitol wore silk, it seemed. The silkworm trees had been planted and were taking root, and all the silk from across the land had been brought in and painstakingly woven and dyed, so that by the time of the wedding, the capitol would be adorned in nothing but the finest silks, worn by everyone, in the appropriate color for their social class.

Cangjie had been put out of his lodging inside the palace by the time they arrived, months after the Yellow Emperor and his party had returned. His place had been taken by a large group of workers for the wedding, almost twelve women crammed into the room that Cangjie had used for himself alone. He discovered that all twelve women were attendants for the Yellow Emperor's bride, keeping her every need met all day long as the wedding preparations proceeded.

"Am I to leave the palace?" Cangjie asked the director of boarding in the southern wing of the palace.

"I'm afraid so, Master Cangjie," said the director with a bow. "But we have made arrangements for you out in the city."

When he arrived at the house where he was to stay, a modest and small place on a clean, well-kept street, Cangjie found a woman crying and her husband trying to console her as they hobbled out of their door, a guard from the palace pushing them.

"But we are honest people!" shouted the man. "We made the sandals on the Yellow Emperor's very feet!"

"You are expelled by order of the Yellow Emperor to make room for important guests for the wedding," the guard said again.

"Please, please!" shouted Cangjie, running up to them. "I am the guest scheduled to stay here. I ask that you do not make them leave. I am happy to sleep outside rather than put this family out of their home."

"Not possible," said the guard. "They are not of the proper class for the wedding."

Cangjie watched the guard shove the old couple down the street. When they had gotten far enough away that they were merely small dots in Cangjie's vision, the guard turned and walked back toward the palace. Cangjie moped inside.

There he saw mounds of sandals as tall as him, and walls covered in rough rope lengths and hides and strange metal tools he had never seen before. He looked at the mountain of sandals and pulled out a pair. He had only rarely put on sandals, as he had grown up going barefoot and preferred for his feet to communicate with the earth. But these were unlike any sandals Cangjie had ever put on. The ropes did not cut the tops of his feet, and the animal hides against the bottoms on his feet were soft and supple, like the gentle moss and soft mud along the edge of a creek.

Cangjie felt there must be something to learn from these masterful craftsmen.

He ran out into the street, looking far along in the direction the old couple had gone. He bent over and tightened the ropes quickly, then ran after them. When he caught them, Cangjie was out of breath.

"Please, come back to your home. I will merely be your humble guest until the wedding is over."

"But, we are not of the proper class. We are but sandal makers," the woman cried.

"Very well," Cangjie said. "Come to your home, where, for this short time, you will be *my* guests."

It was merely a shift in the words, but it was enough to convince the old couple to agree.

As the days passed, more and more people came to the capitol. A large camp of commoners and the poor was set up in the open spaces and the woods outside of the city walls, where all through the day and well into the night could be heard much celebrating and singing, and some occasional loud words of arguing.

Lying in the bed of his hosts late in the nights, Cangjie wondered how a word said loudly in arguments or drunken singing, if it was captured, would be different than the same word said when happy or in a secret whisper. Was a word always just that word?

More and more preparations for the ceremony were made. A large tent was erected beside the palace. Exotic animals from distant lands were marched in through the capitol. Horse dung was shoveled from every street the moment it hit the dirt. Singers and dancers arrived and put on shows throughout the capitol. Performers arrived, some as official participants, but many others from the tiny villages where they were strange, eccentric men who threw knives with shocking accuracy or danced atop tiny platforms balanced high in the air on whittled and decorated logs.

Each day, as more people arrived, Cangjie took the sandals of his hosts out into the street to sell to the travelers. And each evening, he returned home with the oddest assortment of items in his satchel that he'd bartered for the sandals—knobby purple vegetables from far out in the land, a black-feathered chicken, fine porcelain cups and copper bracelets, and many trinkets and pieces of sparkling rock that Cangjie accepted out of pure amusement.

The old couple were always grateful for whatever was in Cangjie's satchel. They seemed more and more intrigued by the odd and surprising things that came to them from across the vast land that they now lived in, united in peace. They seemed to not believe that the world could contain so many things.

Each night they worked until the last moment of light, and sometimes even into the dark, to make enough sandals to send back out into that vast world. Cangjie sat in the room each night and admired them at their work.

Finally, late one night, he had a question that seemed to come to him out of nowhere. He watched the old man etching into the wooden platform on the bottom of the sandal. He carved grooves and swirls and intricate patterns, tedious and time-consuming work.

"Why do you do this?" Cangjie asked. "It is merely the bottom of the sandal, that touches the earth, not the foot. No one will see this part of the sandal."

"Ah, they will not see this on the sandal, but on the earth others will see that one of our sandals has been there before them," said the old man. "And perhaps they will want to make such a mark themselves, with a sandal of their own. Who knows?"

Cangjie laughed and the old man laughed, and the old woman smiled and kept humming her ancient song and weaving together the ropes.

On the day of the Yellow Emperor's wedding, Cangjie joined the crowds streaming toward the palace, trying to find a spot with a view. He was standing quite contentedly in the middle of the street, surrounded by his fellow citizens from across the land,

and from their vantage point up on a little hill it seemed that Cangjie could see the ceremony in all its glory, though the Yellow Emperor would be nothing more than a tiny speck visible from a distance in his now-famous yellow robe.

But then a palace guard who was passing through the crowd with a menacing look and a large sword spotted him.

"Master Cangjie! Why is it that you are here, so far away and out with the people? You are to come with me," said the guard. Cangjie had no time to claim his spot there in the road. The guard grabbed him by the arm and led him through the crowd, shouting and threatening with his sword so that the people parted like water around a protruding rock. Cangjie found himself brought right up to the front, seated in a grand and intricately-carved chair right in the front row, mere feet from the Yellow Emperor and his bride.

All around him, Cangjie could see, were artists feverishly trying to capture the moment. Painters made scratchy sketches of the palace and the layout of the guests. Musicians listened closely to the thrum of the crowd and the royal songs of the prelude, to make their own commemoration song. Even Wei was off to the side, looking in every direction for details to remember, to pack away in his beautiful mind and later regale the people across the land with when he sang the poem of the great Yellow Emperor's wedding. Through an open doorway, Cangjie could see the dozen recordkeepers, peering out through the opening and tying knots feverishly to commemorate whatever it was they had in mind at the moment.

The ceremony was grand and long, as Cangjie supposed a royal wedding must be. The Yellow Emperor thought of himself as a man of the people, and this lavish event was like a gift to them, celebrating this new world they would create together.

Yet for long stretches of the service, Cangjie felt his mind wander off, to distant lands he had visited during the great battles, to his home village where his wife waited for news of the royal wedding. And to his task, which he had been at work on for so many months now, and which he was no closer to finding a solution for.

Wei was convinced that there was no need to trap words, that we had no right to words that we did not make, and no right for our words to last longer than the moment we make them.

But Cangjie wasn't sure he agreed with his old friend.

Watching the Yellow Emperor and Leizu during the ceremony from his seat in the front row, Cangjie saw that they talked the whole time. Quietly, they spoke to each other, ignoring the officiant. They told jokes and smiled, they complimented each other, they laughed at the hoopla surrounding them.

At one moment, the Yellow Emperor leaned down and whispered something into his bride's ear. She smiled, then stood on her tiptoes and whispered something back into the Yellow Emperor's ear. He smiled back at her.

Cangjie heard nothing of the exchange, but something about it thrilled him.

That moment, a moment of words, could never be captured by any artists. No painting could do it. Not even Wei could. Certainly there was a knot or two about it, but those had failed the instant they were tied.

The words had a power that the knots, and even the art, didn't. Cangjie saw that happen. He understood then why it was crucial that he succeed in his task.

For if there was a way for him to capture the words, he could make his feelings known to his wife, though far away from her, and there would not have to be a messenger to carry his words and interpret them. No other person would even know them at all.

If there were a way to capture words, everyone could know the story of this ceremony, from beginning to end, not just one moment captured in a painting or drawing, or one moment listening to a traveling poet. The story would be there, always, for all people.

Cangjie saw what the Yellow Emperor had understood from the beginning. To capture the words would be a miracle. The words could be sent without their speaker, like a message without a messenger. The soldier could send his love to his family. The traveler could update his daughter as to when he would return home.

And Cangjie himself could send his wife the words that would explain his feelings.

More than anything, Cangjie wanted to do this.

As he watched the Yellow Emperor and his bride, Cangjie missed his own wife more terribly than he ever had. He wanted to tell her this, tell her that he loved her dearly. He wanted to tell her how hard he worked at this impossible task, so that he would return home to her more quickly.

If there were such a way to capture his thoughts and his words, he would send them to her. He wanted more than anything to give her this message.

But how? Cangjie felt again the rush of terror at the magnitude of his task. How can the words of our heart and our mind and our mouth be more than what they are as we express them? How can words be made permanent, like a drawing, like a knot? How can they be captured, like a butterfly or a silkworm?

Cangjie did not know. But he did know he had to send the message of his feelings to his wife. And since there was no way to capture the words yet, he took it upon himself to deliver it.

Late in the night, as another round of roasted tapir was being served, another song was struck up by a traveling band of musicians, another limb added to a roaring bonfire to keep the revelers warm and in a celebratory state, Cangjie snuck out of the old couple's home. The celebration was set to go on for a month, during which time Cangjie was sure he would not be missed.

Before he left, he took off his luxurious silk robe and wrapped himself in his old hemp blanket and tied it with a sash. He folded the robe in a neat square and left it on his sleeping mat.

Then he made a gift of everything he had with him. Everything he had in the world, almost. He left his fine bone comb and all of the valuable stones he had in his purse, all of the bartered goods that he had intended to take back with him to his lodging in the palace. He left the ornate box the Yellow Emperor had given him, as a token of his admiration for the task he was undertaking.

Cangjie stole out into the night, where it was as light as day in the firelight of the feasting and celebrating. He had with him only his rough robe and his sash and a pair of the old couple's sandals, which he had grown quite fond of over the week. He could make it back to his village much quicker with the sandals on, then return and redouble his efforts to complete his charge and capture the words.

But something came to Cangjie as he walked away from the palace and the throngs of revelers began to thin out. The world became darker there on the edges of the capitol city, in the messenger's moment before the light began to bleed across the eastern horizon.

He saw a poor beggar asleep next to a trash heap, where he had been looking for anything of value. Cangjie took off the sandals and tucked them under the poor man's arm, and made his way out onto the dark road in his bare feet.

For, why should Cangjie leave the print of his good friend's sandals? He was off to capture the words. Why not leave his own foot's unique imprint along his way?

The Ghosts Howl

Winter was coming on fast now. Cangjie could feel it in his feet as he walked back toward his village. He could see the trees starting to slow themselves, the leaves curling slightly inward. Cangjie feared Yinglong could bring rain to the cold air and cause a great snow to blind him to his direction, so he stayed on the road along the way, for he wanted to journey home with speed like the dragon in flight.

It had been a winter's journey that had won the Yellow Emperor his great victory over Chi You. Cangjie's messengers brought him news that the Jiuli tribes were settling in place to wait out the cold season. The Yellow Emperor decided to advance upon them. The idea felt wrong in the bones of every soldier and general in the army. For many lifetimes, nomadic people stayed still to conserve energy during the cold season. But the Yellow Emperor delivered a great speech, wielding his sword over his head and promising a peaceful land where the people—all people—would have a better life.

And the nomadic peoples had moved through that cold and defeated the great Jiuli army so soundly it was as if that tribe had never existed.

The Yellow Emperor's promise, *for all people,* haunted Cangjie as he traveled back toward his village and the comfort of his wife. In many ways, it was coming true. The Yellow Emperor had brought peace. The silkworm trees were taking root in the earth all across the land, and Cangjie saw more and more fine robes of silk worn by fellow travelers along the road.

Cangjie understood now why the Yellow Emperor wanted a way to make a record of words. They were living in a magical time of peace and progress. He understood that, when the poets sing songs of the past, it is never the magical, peaceful times that make up the story.

But this time *must* be made permanent with a record.

And though he feared that the heavens would bring a wrath of flood and famine for the way men were behaving like gods and making their stories permanent, Cangjie did not want to fail the Yellow Emperor in this magical time.

Cangjie was even starting to believe his task was possible, though the way eluded him like the invisible spirits and gods that traveled the land much as he did.

The answer was there, somewhere, calling out to him. If he could only grasp it.

The other path to his answer was to wait and let it come to him seemingly out of nowhere, like a nearly-forgotten memory. But Cangjie had always been a man of action and movement. He preferred to hunt his solution.

So with each traveler he met along the road, he talked. He learned of new things in each village, like plants that artists were mashing into a mud that was in bold colors like nature, and strange fruits brought in at the ports from distant countries they now engaged in trade. He heard that the Yellow Emperor's bride, Leizu, created a method of changing the color of silk robes by boiling a vat of water with combinations of plants. Cangjie heard the robes turned the color of the sun, or the sky. They could be as green as a new leaf or dark as the moonless night.

Each time he spoke with someone new, Cangjie was thinking about words. Was there a way to use a net or a gourd to grab his new friend's words out of the air? Was there a way, like a painting, to make them dry and permanent, so they could speak to others without their speaker? Was there a way this traveler's news from across this vast land, with such distant parts, could spread in many directions at once, if the words did not have to come from the traveler each time?

When he stopped in the evenings, Cangjie made himself ask for shelter at a house along the road, rather than stay out in the open air as he preferred. He asked each time how his hosts kept records, for not everywhere was there an unlimited store of rope to tie in knots. And there were many methods he had not thought of—notches in wooden planks, scratches in flat faces of rock, tiny rocks in piles.

Cangjie was amazed at the genius he saw in the solutions that seemed to come as natural as sunshine to the people that showed him their record-keeping methods.

Yet when he told them of his task, capturing words to make record of them, his hosts and his fellow travelers shook their heads and looked at him as if he were a lowly trickster out to bamboozle them. They told him it was impossible. There was no need to capture words, either.

As Cangjie rested on the side of the road one day, he sighed as he rubbed his dirty and calloused feet. Perhaps they were right. Perhaps his task was futile because it was needless.

He heard the thum-thum-thum of a horse's hooves approaching on the dirt road and felt it in his back through the earth well before he could see it. Here would be another traveler on horseback that Cangjie could approach, hoping for a new idea to open his mind about trapping words in place forever.

"Why bother?" asked Cangjie aloud, to the road and the forest. "What will this man know that no others have?" He listened to the hooves as they approached yet closer, but heard also a strange creak and clack in time with them. Cangjie dreaded the man's passing, for like every traveler he encountered, they would each ask about their journeys and their destinations, and whether they were in need of supplies or had anything they would like to exchange. Cangjie did not feel like sharing words with this man, or any man, at the moment.

But when the horse came into view, it was as if the

gods had opened their veil on another secret. For behind the horse was a large wooden box on wheels also made of wood, a large construction that seemed to move at the same speed as the trotting horse. Cangjie had never fathomed of a cart that could move faster than a man could push or pull it.

The traveler slowed when he approached, and Cangjie saw that the wooden box on wheels was attached to the horse by long, strong wooden arms and smartly-placed ropes around the horse's middle. He could only gape at the genius of it. He had no words at all.

"Friend," said the older man who stood inside the cart. He smiled and showed a mouth with only three teeth. "To where do you go?"

Cangjie admired the astounding simplicity of the idea to lash a cart to a horse. Inside the cart with the man was a satchel full of oats and hay for the horse and a bladder of water for them both. There were other items that the man did not have to carry in a pack, as Cangjie did—a blanket, his hunting weapons, items he'd traded for along the road.

Cangjie stared at the horse and cart like it was the first time he'd ever set foot on the soil. The invention opened strange new worlds right before Cangjie's eyes as he looked the arrangement over. Fruits and plants could be carried from one part of the land to another without spoiling. Whole silkworm trees could be transported and planted with their own roots and earth. One horse could carry a whole family.

He realized he'd been silent for longer than he knew. The man in the cart was still smiling at him.

"To my village of Zhou, above the Yellow River," said Cangjie. "And you, Friend?"

"The capitol!" the nearly toothless man said.

"Ah! To sell this fine invention, then? You will leave there a rich man." Cangjie bowed.

"No, Friend, this cart is a gift to the Yellow Emperor. But yes, I nevertheless hope to leave a rich man!" He smiled and laughed, full of an energy that Cangjie had not seen in weeks along the road.

"Come," the man said, waving Cangjie toward him. "Climb in. You are but an afternoon away from home and I shall be glad to take you there."

"I cannot accept. It would trouble you too much by slowing your journey. Surely the Yellow Emperor desires you in the capitol very soon."

"Bah," said the man. "I am now a faster traveler than almost everyone in the world. What's an extra afternoon?"

Cangjie climbed aboard in a cloud of emotion. He felt anger and jealousy at this poor and toothless man completing a task for the Yellow Emperor and being richly rewarded for it. He felt admiration and wonder at the simple solution. He felt hope that the solution to his own charge from the Yellow Emperor might be so simple, that it could arrive around a bend in the road just as this horse and cart had.

They began to move and Cangjie felt the strangest sensation, standing still and upright while moving ahead with the wind in his face and hair. He took the bone out of his hair and let it down to float in the breeze. The toothless man smiled at the expression of joy and fear Cangjie knew he wore on his face.

For a moment, Cangjie thought about all the people he had met along the road before this man, the ones who told him there was no need for captured words. He couldn't help thinking that he understood something about words that they didn't.

They did not know that the need for them to be captured even existed. They did not understand what they themselves most needed.

Just as Cangjie, standing in a cart that he did not know existed a mere few moments before, was now wondering why he never thought of such a thing, and how he had traveled all those years without it.

Cangjie knew down in his bones that his people didn't know they needed captured words because they have yet to have them. Once Cangjie was successful, they will wonder how they ever used words that were merely moments of sound.

Every traveler they passed looked at them with amazement, like they were mountain spirits in the flesh. Every hut they whizzed by suddenly burst open with people running out to the road to see this cart that moved with the speed of a horse. Little children begged to ride in the cart, and the old man would pack in as many as he could and trot them along for a short distance before shooing them away and returning to the journey.

The old man never stopped smiling his toothless smile.

Cangjie's respect for the old man only grew, the longer they went. It was thrilling to stand still and yet move in the cart. Cangjie's feet, for so long accustomed to feeling the earth beneath them, were unsure on the moving platform. He had relied on them to keep him safe through many dangerous years, and soon enough they adjusted to the bumps and lurches of the movement and Cangjie could balance without concentrating. It was as if he had ridden in this horse cart his entire life.

The old man also had no trouble balancing, despite

being as thin as a bird in his legs. Cangjie thought that he perhaps actually *had* ridden in horse carts his entire life.

"Friend?" Cangjie asked. "How did you come to make this invention?"

The old man smiled even bigger, and Cangjie wondered if he would smile as much, were he to ever be able to complete his task. He wondered if the old man might be able to help him, somehow.

"Got old," the old man said. He smiled and looked forward at the horse's rear end, as if that was all there was to the answer. But Cangjie was accustomed to murky conversations from all his years speaking in a messenger's code.

"What is it that you use the cart for?" he asked.

"Stonework, Friend. I build walls and fences. But I became too old to carry stones the great distance from where we dig them out. So I designed a way for my horse to carry them."

Cangjie felt sadness in his belly again. For this was another great advancement brought about by obvious necessity. There was nothing of gods or magical creatures behind it.

"Is that how the Emperor discovered your cart, from your stonework?" Cangjie asked, hopefully.

"Accident!" the old man laughed. "I was collecting stones from the riverbank one day several winters ago, when the Emperor and many more people came along the road. I did not know it was the Emperor, because my village had received no messengers to say we had a new Emperor, but his guards came down to me from the road and ordered me to stop, and then the Emperor himself came down to the riverbank. I thought I was about to be executed for taking the rock!"

He smiled again, as big as the sun, and looked forward at his horse.

"The Emperor, he was astonished. He kept bowing to me, and I bowed in return, until I had to lay down on the damp earth because my old back could move no lower. Ha ha! He left two men to study the cart with me, and the party moved on. By the time the new moon came, a messenger arrived with ideas for the cart from the Emperor. The messenger told me that I was to incorporate these ideas and use my own, and when I was done to bring the cart to the palace. So I do!" he laughed.

"Friend, you will be richly rewarded. You will spend the rest of your life in silk robes," Cangjie told him.

"What is this 'silk' you speak of?" the old man asked. Cangjie noticed that he was wearing animal fur, and he smiled at the old man and the world and the way we know some things but never fathom of the things others know. What is normal for one man is not for any other.

"And is this to be colored in fine paints and embedded with precious stones to be used by the Yellow Emperor?" asked Cangjie.

"Perhaps this cart will," the old man said. "But the Emperor's first demand was that any man in any village with any regular supplies must be able to build this cart. I must make it simple, you see. So I use only the wood from fallen trees, and saws and pins and rope. He wants all people across the land to have carts. My carts! Ha!"

The two of them in the cart crested a hill which was at the top of a valley. Across the valley was Cangjie's village. This was usually one of Cangjie's most thrilling moments as a traveler, to see his home from across the beautiful, lush green expanse with the river like a great snake along its belly. He could see smoke trails from the small fires drying meats, the women carrying blankets, the men hunting and foraging along the steep slopes down toward the river.

But here in this moment, Cangjie did not think of them in his usual way. He was astounded, thinking of his fellow villagers. His wife. His son. And all the fellow villagers and wives and sons and daughters in every village across the vast land, from the poorest beggars to the most honored royalty.

For Cangjie's task was not just for him to find a solution for the Yellow Emperor. Like the magical cart that he floated upon, Cangjie's captured words must be something to be used by every person in every village with any regular supplies.

The old man was smiling at him. "That is your village, yes?"

Cangjie nodded. He had gotten into the cart in search of an idea or a hint that would help him discover a way to trap words in place forever.

Instead, Cangjie saw his task all anew again. The cart

and horse and the two men began down the steep road into the valley and picked up speed toward the bottom, and with a great dizziness at the way they were being pulled faster and faster, Cangjie looked at the old man. Like him, Cangjie must find a simple solution. And like the cart that pulled them faster and faster, moving them though they took no step of their own, Cangjie's success with the task would somehow feel magical, were he to ever succeed.

He looked over at the man, who smiled with his three teeth. Cangjie was in awe.

It was only after their grand arrival into his village, where the children spotted them a great distance down the road and ushered them in like a foaming and churning wave to the shore, that Cangjie finally began to calm his mind. With everyone so intrigued by the new and wondrous invention of the cart, Cangjie did not have to stop and tell them of his adventures and the things he'd seen.

Over the years, Cangjie had come to resent this ritual when he returned to his village. His neighbors and friends were amazed by his tales, yet they themselves would never venture beyond the clearing on the outskirts of the village or the banks of the river below them. Their still lives frustrated Cangjie, for they had all come from nomadic ancestors who were always moving for their next meal, next season, next possibility.

So Cangjie slipped away when the crowd surrounded the old man and the cart, and walked back to his own house with a strange buzzing numbness in his feet. The houses were deserted with his arrival. His neighbors were certainly planning a celebration for the arrival of the horse and cart, because, as Cangjie had seen on the road, the usefulness of it was instantly apparent to even the poorest laborer.

Yet he had not seen his wife anywhere among the throng. That meant she had seen or heard of his impending arrival from someone who'd spotted them across the valley. And that she was awaiting him in their small home.

For it was indeed small, as Cangjie saw it again, not fifty paces away. It surprised him how dirty it seemed, after living in the palace for many nights. Even in comparison with the sandal makers' home, it looked ragged and poor.

He wondered if, were he to succeed in the Emperor's mission, he would be rewarded with a grander life than he could imagine.

Instantly, Cangjie was ashamed of the thought. He tried to banish it from his mind as he approached his door. When he rounded the corner, the thought flew away like a forgotten word, because his son was sitting on the step, looking out across the lush valley.

At least, it seemed to be his son. It looked like Shoyu, but he was much larger and longer. His arms were muscled, his face as angular as chiseled stone. Had Cangjie been away so long that his son had become a man?

"Father," his son said, standing and bowing. His voice was much deeper, but had a note of sadness in it. Cangjie bowed in return.

"Mother is inside," his son said. Cangjie thought he

should stay and share words with his son, a man he hardly knew who was his own blood. But his wife was there, mere steps away, and Cangjie could not control his desire for her. He would speak with Shoyu later.

His wife welcomed Cangjie into their bed. He was overtaken with his passions and made love to her in a frenzied hurry, after which they held each other quietly, and stroked each others' bodies as if to confirm they were real. Together they drifted in and out of sleep, and then made love again, more tenderly and slowly and personally, as night drew over the village.

Only then did they begin to speak words to each other. They could hear the celebration beginning, the children squealing as they took dizzying rides along in the horse cart. And Cangjie told his wife where he had been for all these months, what it was that the Yellow Emperor was requiring him to create. He lamented how his task seemed so impossible in comparison to robes of silk and carts pulled by horses.

"What is silk?" his wife asked. As Cangjie explained it and the other things he had learned, he realized he had seen so much and traveled so far, he had no idea what was normal in the land anymore.

Cangjie did not feel like he was living in peaceful and boring times.

"I have been gone too long for my own good, and now that winter is coming on, I will be able to stay here at home with you and rest and think. Perhaps then the solution will come to me."

Cangjie could see his beautiful wife thinking over

everything he'd told her. He could see the words forming in her mind.

For a moment, Cangjie wished that he could go back to when he first met her, when they were young and poor and free. Before he left her unknowingly pregnant, before his years away carrying messages, before he returned to his village and was given servants, before he became burdened by this task. He wished he knew nothing of what he had come to know.

"Master Cangjie, Husband, Great Communicator," she said, finally, "you must leave again in the morning. Do you not see the greatness of your task? How much your success at it will change the world for all times?"

"No, I will stay," Cangjie said. "I have been searching for an answer, and none has come. I can do just as well staying here with you and sharing our bed and not finding the answer, too."

She smiled at him. But she also said no with her body.

"Dear Cangjie, in your travels, did you yet hear of the Yellow Emperor's latest victory?" she asked. Cangjie shook his head no, and his wife turned her body toward him on their mat. She smiled.

"You see," she said, "we have had several poets travel through and tell the story. Each poet tells it better than the one before. It seems there was a great giant named Xing Tian, loyal to Yan still all these years after his defeat. He approached the palace walls and challenged the Yellow Emperor to a duel. It was a heroic fight with swords and axes, and the poets go on and on about each swing and dodge. But in the end, with a trick, the Yellow Emperor distracted the giant and cut off his head."

"Oh, blessed Emperor!" said Cangjie.

"Dear husband, you mustn't believe everything the poets say. For the Yellow Emperor buried the giant's head inside a mountain with a single stroke of his axe. And the giant Xing Tian refused to be defeated. When he could not find his head, he began to use the nipples upon his chest as unseeing eyes and his navel as an unopening mouth. And as a headless giant with a face on his torso, he battles wildly and blindly with his sword wherever he goes."

"What a foolish giant," Cangjie said. "I wonder if the poets' story is true."

"Foolish giant, perhaps," said his wife. "But it is more foolish to wonder at the truth of the story and yet be blind to its meaning."

Cangjie did not know what his wife meant. With a look in his eyes that needed no words, he begged her to explain. She lay on her back and looked up at their woven roof that never leaked, and she spoke.

"Dear Cangjie," she said. "You are the greatest man in the village, and you are larger than it. You will find no answers here. I, too, will miss you. But I do not want to be the one preventing you from succeeding in your task to capture the words. It is too important. You must be like Xing Tian. Unrelenting and constantly battling and refusing to admit defeat."

Cangjie rolled over in bed and looked up at the roof.

He felt that heavy weight upon him again, the impossible burden of his task and the sting of his wife's words because they were correct.

"I wish we could go back to being who we were long ago when we first met," Cangjie said.

She smiled. "Those were wonderful days."

"Yet they are gone. As distant as a drop of water in a river becomes."

"And yet," she said, as she rolled over on top of his chest and kissed it, "does not that drop of water come back, and fall from the sky as rain? If you find a way to trap words forever, we could tell the words of what we do each day, and go back to them later. We could go back to those days in our mind. Someday, when we are old and have only three teeth and must ride around in horse carts because we are too fragile to walk, we can return to this day, this happy moment when we are together, through the words we capture about it."

His wife, his beautiful wife. In all his travels and his searching for his task, Cangjie had been looking at it the wrong way, always. He had been looking for the solution, but had never once thought about how he would use the solution he found.

Cangjie was finding a way to tell his own story. He would not have to leave it to the poets to preserve him through time. And the world dawned new, again, for him.

She was sitting up and putting on her rough woven robe. Cangjie cursed himself for not bringing her fine silk from the capitol. He felt great sorrow that she did not even know of the luxury she did not have.

"You must take Shoyu with you," she said, her back to Cangjie.

"Shoyu? Traveling with a boy would greatly hinder me in my task," Cangjie said.

"Shoyu is no longer a boy. He is a young man now, as silly and foolish as we were in the days you yearn to return to." She was standing up now and Cangjie could still see in her that young woman walking uphill on the road as he walked down into the valley all those winters ago and saw her beauty for the first time.

She looked out to where Shoyu might be, at the feast in the center of the village.

"He is not so carefree as we were," she said. "He is with great sadness."

"Why? Has he not everything he needs here?"

"That is the problem. He has nothing to do, no requirements to keep himself alive. So he flings himself at every girl in the village. He is in love with a particular one, but he thinks he cannot marry her because we are of a higher class since you returned here as a hero who stood at the side of the Yellow Emperor."

Cangjie remembered how the palace had felt like a cage.

He had not asked for the promotions and elevations he'd received in his life. He was merely a messenger, was good at his job, and did it to make a peaceful, better life for his family.

Yet was his son's life better, for all of Cangjie's work?

Was it a better life for a father to not know his own son?

She was leaving the room now. "I will have the servants begin preparations for you both to leave in the morning with the man on the horse cart."

Cangjie watched the empty door with his heart sinking. It rose again like a flower upon the first sign of Spring, when she returned to the doorway.

"And the next time you return, after being successful in your task, I will never send you away again," she said.

She smiled, and Cangjie cried in the joy of such a thought.

The old man and the cart carried Cangjie and Shoyu far from the village by midday, when Cangjie decided it was best to depart their ride and walk along the road. They were getting closer to the capitol, and Cangjie did not want to go there yet. He had a nervous feeling in his stomach of what the Emperor would say as he admonished him for his failure at the simple task he'd been given.

His legs felt funny as they began the work they'd always done, walking along the road, because of the vibrations in the cart. But what felt the most strange was walking alongside Shoyu, who was now a bit taller than Cangjie, even though Shoyu hung his head in sadness and said absolutely no words.

"Shoyu, I must tell you something," Cangjie said after walking many paces along the road. There seemed to be no village nearby and no other travelers, so there was no way for Cangjie to approach his mission at this time. "It seems I have been away so much that I have missed your childhood. You have become a man, and I didn't even know it."

Shoyu didn't say anything, yet again. He looked

down at the dirt and stones of the road. Cangjie watched the great length of his strides, the bounce in his foot against the earth.

Cangjie realized that he had not been much older than Shoyu when he set off from the village to join the Yellow Emperor and defeat the invading tribes. He'd done that to make his land a better place for the next generations. And yet here was his son at that same age, and with nothing to throw his heart into. The very peace and prosperity Cangjie had fought for had become a burden and a boredom to his son. His heart sank a little.

"Your mother tells me that you are in love with a young woman," Cangjie tried.

"Perhaps my mother shares too many words," Shoyu said.

"You will be respectful of your mother."

"Yes, Father."

They walked many paces in tense silence, then. The forest along the road seemed to be thinning and they were walking down a gentle slope into another valley.

"I understand, my son, that you feel you are not allowed to marry the one you love," Cangjie finally said.

"She is of the poorest clan in all the village," Shoyu said. "And we are its most honored family. The village is full of stares and whispers when we are together. So we are never together."

"Have you told her of your feelings?" Cangjie asked.

"We are never together. So I cannot."

Words, again. If Cangjie was successful, Shoyu could send the girl a message and make his feelings known. He tried to think of what to tell him to make it bearable until then.

"You know, the Yellow Emperor recently married a young woman. And she was not of his same social class," Cangjie tried.

"But *no one* is of the Emperor's class," Shoyu said.

"Yes, exactly. Do you think the Yellow Emperor was concerned with what people would say if he married below his class? Because he was in love?"

Shoyu said nothing again, and merely looked down at the path they followed.

Ahead, Cangjie could see a clearing with a slow stream on the far end. There would be a nice open parcel of short wild plants and full sun where the two of them could rest and warm their bodies in the open light. He was beginning to feel hungry and hoped for some vegetation to forage or perhaps some wildlife to hunt. Cangjie quickened his pace slightly.

So did Shoyu, who seemed to see something Cangjie did not. Shoyu was looking at the clearing, too, and broke out of his fast walk into a run.

"Father!" he called. "You must see!" Shoyu was pointing into the clearing, and Cangjie hurried to his side. He looked out into the open expanse and his mind could not decipher what his eyes saw.

There was much vegetation, but it was not the wild greenery that Cangjie was expecting. The plants were in row after row, in lines as straight as an arrow's flight, set side by side like sticks laid ready for weaving. Each line had a great many plants in it, all of the same kind, and after several lines began a new kind of plant. In between each line was a path that was full of footprints, left by a man or woman, or many men and women, who took great care of these orderly lines of plants.

Cangjie thought back to the beginning of this strange journey, when he first learned of his task to capture the words. When the Yellow Emperor had first told him about it, he had been in a magnificent garden at the palace, where he was overwhelmed at the way the garden was making beautiful order out of the chaos of nature.

But this was a greater order than even the most beautiful garden.

The lines seemed to extend the entire length of the clearing, and everything that came out of the ground seemed to have been there for a specific purpose.

Shoyu ran down from the road and into the lines of vegetation. He reached down and pulled out a carrot as long as his forearm and laughed loudly. He bounded over a few rows and plucked an eggplant off at its stem.

All the plants were for eating.

The wonder and terror of what he was seeing came upon Cangjie like a dragon swooping out of the sky and shredding him with its claws. Each row was full of things to eat, right here by the village, in order, not out in the wild chaos of the woods where men had to scramble and scrounge for things to bring back to the village to eat.

Shoyu seemed to understand this, too. He was laughing and running along the rows, peering into them to see what grew next.

"You there!" came a voice from across the clearing. A middle-aged man stepped deftly across the rows towards them, brandishing a sword. "You must leave! If you continue to steal, you will be punished severely!"

Cangjie hurried down and met the man. "My son means you no harm. We are merely out on a mission for the Yellow Emperor and we have never before seen such a thing as this."

"Master Cangjie?" said the man.

"You know me?"

"The Emperor spoke many times of you when he was here," the man said. "Yours is a great mission, he said."

Cangjie felt that nervous twinge in his stomach. "The Yellow Emperor was here?"

"Isn't it clear that he was? This was his idea," the man said, waving his arm out at the straight lines of food, all together in one expanse, that sprung forth willingly from the earth.

"What do you call this?" asked Cangjie.

"Farming!" the man said, smiling. "Will you not stay and share some of the bounty of this land?"

Cangjie was about to decline the generous offer to eat the fruits of the earth, when Shoyu came loping up to them.

"Father! We can do such a thing at our village! We can make the food come to us rather than hunting for it in the valley and never having enough," he said. Cangjie was astounded. He had not yet thought that such an orderly feat was possible anywhere else in the land but where they stood.

"May I stay here and learn how?" Shoyu asked. "Then, when I go back, I can leave my mark as the man who brought the food from the earth."

"Farming, it is called," Cangjie told his son. "I do not know if you are able to take on an apprentice," he said to the man.

"By decree of the Yellow Emperor, I am to take on anyone who requests it, and teach others who are reluctant, as well!" said the man. "And anyone I teach must return to their village and do the same. It is the Yellow Emperor's command that farming be done in every village across the land, for all the people to have the bounty of the earth come to them."

Cangjie smiled. He looked at Shoyu, at the ambition and joy in his eyes.

"Good Sir, we accept your offer to taste the fruits of this farming. And then I must continue with the task the Yellow Emperor has given me. And I will leave my son, Shoyu, in your care."

The man bowed and Cangjie bowed in return. Shoyu bowed to them both, and they did so, and there was a great round of bowing in the field amidst the farming. As they walked in toward the village to eat, Cangjie leaned in to his son and spoke softly.

"Shoyu, if you bring this farming to our village, I do think you can marry any woman you choose. It is likely you will have many wives."

Shoyu walked beside Cangjie, but seemed to float a small bit above the earth as he did so.

With a full belly and a broken heart, Cangjie walked away from the village where he first learned of farming. The world was changing too fast, almost as if he could feel it moving beneath his feet. Shoyu would be working the land for the next few seasons, earning his way by growing his own food. Then, Shoyu would return to teach farming to all their neighbors, and he would forever change their village. He would be part of this fast change in the world.

Cangjie also knew that the next time he saw Shoyu, he would be even more of a man, and would probably have fallen in love with another girl. Perhaps he would even be married. Perhaps he would have a son of his own by then. His son would change quickly, as well.

The world was leaving Cangjie. The thought weighed heavier than any messenger's burden. He began to put his feet one in front of the other and move simply because that was what his body knew how to do. He moved great distances over many moons, an old messenger with no message.

He felt tired deep down in his bones as he walked the road. For weeks he wandered, and though he knew where he was, Cangjie was lost. The cold grew stronger with each step he took. Birds gathered shelter for the winter season. Rodents grew fat for hiding themselves away. Trees shed their leaves and the winds blew like a thousand arrows.

Cangjie felt he was not on earth, but was descending into Diyu, deep within the eighteen hells.

With all of the new things he had seen since he had taken on this task for the Yellow Emperor, from fine silk robes to fast carts behind horses to food that came up from the ground just where you wished it to, he felt that his efforts had been a failure.

He had become an old man and had wasted his few remaining days on an impossible task.

To capture words! Were such a thing possible, wouldn't someone have done it already? Should it not have been created naturally, out of someone's necessity?

Cangjie had failed. He knew it. Even his son knew it, and so he'd abandoned Cangjie to take up the farming trade and make his own mark on the world, separate from his father's.

The only thing he had left to live for was his wife, but even she would be unhappy to see him. She understood how important his task was, and how it would change the world. And the next time they met, all she would see would be an old man who hadn't been up to the task, had not had the strength to change the world any further.

This thought made Cangjie's legs go limp. He

stumbled to the edge of the road and sat down, looking out into a plain with trees and bushes, a mountain far off in the distance. He felt it begin to rain, soft at first and then heavy drops that pelted him like pebbles thrown from the heavens.

Yet Cangjie did not seek shelter beneath any nearby trees. He simply sat and waited on the rain and the cold to mercifully end his life. And if nature did not kill him, he would ask the next traveler along the road the way to the Yellow Emperor's palace, where he would travel and admit his failure, and accept his execution.

It rained, on and on, for what seemed like many days. Cangjie could not tell when the darkness was night and when it was merely the rainclouds. He was certain this was the wrath of both the rainbird Shang-Yang and the rain dragon Shenlong upon him.

Cangjie shivered like a dying animal. He opened his mouth to the sky to wet his parched throat. He lay back in the muddy road, into the tiny streams that formed along its sides, and opened his eyes to see the earth one last time.

But what he saw, he did not expect. Above him, just a way out into the open field, flew a hawk. It came out of the dark grey sky and moved through the air, heading the same direction as Cangjie along the road. But it labored in the hard rain to flap its waterlogged wings.

This was because, Cangjie saw, the hawk was carrying in its claws the leg of some animal, part of a carcass that it had found. But in this rain, the leg proved too heavy to bring back to the nest. The hawk cried out and dropped the leg and then lifted itself higher into the gray mist of the sky until it disappeared.

Cangjie watched the leg fall. It looked like the hindquarter of some animal that walked on all fours.

What he had just seen would be a fitting last image of life on this cruel earth. He would have been perfectly right to close his eyes and wait for his own death. He even did so for a moment.

But then the rain let up to a pleasant patter into the puddles.

And Cangjie made himself sit up, then stand.

He could still see the image of the dead animal's hind leg falling from the hawk's talons to the earth, and he walked out into the plain to find it. He had not gone fifty steps before it appeared right in front of him.

The leg was small and its skin and hair had been removed by the scavengers. Just moments ago, Cangjie had been ready to die, and now he found himself staring at death as it had come to something else. Cangjie wondered what poor animal this was. He could not identify it by looking at the leg.

Perhaps he stared at the leg for hours, thinking, for Cangjie was suddenly startled out of his own thoughts when he heard the unmistakable splashing of footsteps coming along the road. He remembered his promise to ask the next traveler the way to the palace.

But when the traveler came into view, a new thought came to Cangjie, and a whole different set of words came from him as he spoke. It was a hunter on the road, with his bow and quiver and a pelt of animal fur keeping him dry in the rain. Many small animals hung around his waist, limp in their own death as the hunter carried them back to his village.

"Hello, there!" called Cangjie. "Can you help me identify this animal?"

The hunter looked toward the sound of the words and found Cangjie with his eyes. He waved a greeting and left the road to meet Cangjie.

"Friend," he said as he approached, "you look very wet!" He laughed. Cangjie thought this hunter must see a man who does not know the way to stay alive in the wild. And Cangjie did indeed wonder if he was still that man any longer. He did not hold it against the hunter, but merely asked him again.

"Tell me, what kind of animal does this leg come from?"

The hunter glanced at the leg for a mere moment, and seeing that the leg was too eaten to identify, walked instead over to where the animal's hoof had hit the earth first and left an impression in the mud.

"Ah. That is the leg of a pixiu," he said.

"How can you be sure?" Cangjie asked.

"There is no other animal on the earth who makes a hoof print like this one," said the hunter.

"I see," said Cangjie. Each animal has his own print, he thought. How simple.

The rain was still coming down in a gentle fall that splashed across the field and Cangjie looked out at it, at all the animals that had walked across it in the past —he could see them in his mind as he felt his body shivering from the wet and the cold. He envisioned all these animals—they came swirling up out of the ground and he got very dizzy as he stood there, seeing many things. Prints of hooves, prints of claws, prints of the feet of man—Cangjie saw them all on the plain like the earth was a painter's parchment or a wide flat face on a piece of wood.

He could see the impressions like marks, could see which animal was which by the mark it left, as if the mark stood for it. Even the rain left marks in the earth.

A mark for every thing that moves.

Then could there not also be marks for things that did not move, like trees and roads, villages and legendary men now dead?

Cangjie did not feel like he was part of the earth any longer, as all these ideas seemed to envelop him in a blinding light.

For so long he had felt he was grasping at thin air trying to capture words, but now they were so close. He could feel them, like fine silks blowing and whipping all around him in the wind, and if he was quick he might be able to reach out and feel one on his fingertips, brush against the back of his hand, tickle his palm.

The words were close to being captured. He was seeing his answer.

For each thing in heaven and earth, there would be a mark representing it.

The magnitude of what he now understood landed upon his frail and cold body and he fell to his knees in the muddy earth.

"Friend, you are unwell!" shouted the hunter. "You look very pale. We must seek shelter—come with me!"

The hunter said these words, but Cangjie only thought of the marks that must be made to capture them. His mind spun desperately.

Marks, prints, one for every thing he saw, one for everything on the earth, and everything that had ever been on earth or ever would be.

His eyesight became blurry, the colors of the earth drowned away into a muted pool of lights and darks. He felt his back and his arms and legs lose all feeling and become tingling sensations that were unrelated to him.

Because at that moment Cangjie existed only through his mind.

He had done it. He had captured the words. He did not yet know what it would be called, this practice of words being encased forever with a print that stood for each of them. And he did not know how he would make these prints. But he knew now that his story would be told.

His story would be forever.

All the stories that had been told would now be captured. All the deeds of the past, the acts of the moment. They would all be saved, captured, preserved for all time.

Cangjie had invented writing.

He felt the strangest eruption of emotions within his breast when he understood what he had done. He was humbled, and proud, and ashamed, and unworthy.

Even the very earth understood the great shift Cangjie had just caused. The mud beneath him seemed to tilt.

Cangjie heard shrieking and screaming and opened his eyes to the sight of ghosts, hazy wisps like transparent silk spinning out from the earth, howling in terror at Cangjie's invention.

He felt the sky go black and the rain drop heavy for one moment, then become a drizzle of tiny, light pebbles. The pebbles bounced all around him and Cangjie looked closer to see that they were not pebbles but millet grain falling from the sky, coming straight from the gods above to man below.

Everything he knew about this life and this earth would change. It had already changed. This invention had taken it all away, and built it all back again—new and different, yet the same—in an instant.

Cangjie felt himself leaning forward, like a terrible blow had come upon his back. He put his hands out and caught himself on all fours.

He had invented writing, and yet he'd done nothing.

There were so many marks to be made now, so much work yet to be done. Cangjie felt that, even after all of his work so far, he was only just now at the beginning of his impossible task.

"Master, you are very sick!" said the hunter. He heard the hunter's feet splash and squish over to him, and thought about the marks of his feet and the way he might use brush strokes to capture the idea of this hunter, and he felt the hunter's arms go around his sides and pull him upright and carry him back to the road. Cangjie thought he saw a horse cart moving slowly through the mud and ruts of the road, and he thought he saw the hunter waving it down for help.

As they put him in the chariot's bed, everything Cangjie saw was now a small mark that would stand for it.

There were so many marks to make, so much he had yet to do, Cangjie thought as his mind left his body.

The Greatest Poem

When Cangjie awoke, he did not know where he was for a long time. But the former messenger, whose life depended on being keenly aware of his surroundings, didn't care. He felt a chill deep in his muscles and a high fever across his head. So he didn't mind laying on the mat in the strange room there in the dark. He was beneath a warm silk sheet, and his feet had been washed clean, and he felt he could stay there forever.

His clean feet, though, kept coming back into his feverish mind. The longer he lay there, the better he felt, his body warming and his head cooling, and his memory slowly came to him, like the wispy spirits that had emerged from the mud within the field.

The wispy spirits. Yes.

Cangjie remembered the ghosts emerging from the mud, screaming. Why had they come forth?

Then the memory came to him as clear as the midday sun.

The hoofprint, the hunter.

A mark for every thing on the earth.

Cangjie had invented writing.

The thought made him sit up, then jump out of his

comfortable sleeping mat.

It was still dark outside, and Cangjie looked around the room of the kind strangers who had taken him in. He had no time to stay until morning light to thank them, so much was there to do.

For how could there be enough marks? One for every thing, for every person in this land, and in faraway lands, as well? For each village, each vegetable, each bird?

Cangjie gathered the things of his that he could see, and walked slowly and quietly to the door, out into the darkness of the small hour, thinking. He knew that, like the horse cart, his marks must be ones that any man could make, because he knew the Yellow Emperor would want writing to be for all people. This only made it more difficult, only made Cangjie more desperate.

He began walking through the village until he found the road out, which was merely a beaten path through dense foliage. He did not even know exactly which direction he went, only that he had to move, that no answers would come to him while he was enveloped in the comfort of a silk blanket.

It was that most dangerous time of day for messengers, in the morning just before the light came. Cangjie thought back to the day he told his son about this time, back when his son still seemed so young. He thought about his friend Shen, the messenger who did not understand his message, and the long journey he had begun since he was summoned to the palace by the Yellow Emperor.

And as the blue light bled into the horizon, Cangjie thought about that hoof print, the mark for one animal, and how every thing he could see needed its own mark. The task frightened Cangjie as much as it excited him. There was a way for him to capture words simply with a mark, but how? Tiny paintings? Footprints for living things and leaf prints for plants?

Cangjie walked for a great distance in the early morning light thinking of these questions without seeing an answer. Finally, he heard the thumping of horse hooves in the dirt and the familiar wooden clatter of the cart behind it. The idea came to him as if from the gods in the heavens, like the hawk dropping the poor dead animal's leg, and he waved for the cart to stop.

"My friend," Cangjie said to the cart driver, "I am on a mission for the Yellow Emperor, and I must find a poet."

The driver's face went from surprise to utter confusion. It made Cangjie realize that there must be marks for emotions, too, which have no footprint because they are constantly changing.

"In your travels, have you heard of any poets in nearby villages?" Cangjie asked.

"I believe there is one practicing two villages ahead," the driver said. "I am going that way, though I will go further to a village where the fruits of the earth spring forth under the command of a man. Have you heard of such a thing?"

"Yes. It is called farming." The driver's face returned to surprise and wonder. "Will you take me to this poet?"

"Most certainly, Great Master," the driver said, looking wildly at his clothing.

Only then did Cangjie look down and see that he was wearing a robe of silk, put on him by his hosts during the night as he lay sick. They would never see it again. What would be the mark for kindness he could never repay?

Not so long ago, anyone passing them on the road would have flocked to the invention Cangjie and the driver rode upon—for who had seen such a marvel, a cart tied to a horse? Now travelers merely waved at the chariot, if they bothered at all. What had been unimaginable just a short while ago was now as everyday as breath, Cangjie thought as he and the driver floated above the road in the chariot, toward the poet he hoped could help him.

Yet the driver kept asking Cangjie about the orderly way the food came from the ground with this new thing called farming. The plants growing in straight lines, waiting patiently to give their fruits away to the village—it seemed unfathomable that nature could be commanded so.

As they rode along, Cangjie thought about the places that had been farming for several seasons now, and the carts that were just now making their ways along remote roads at the farthest reaches of the land. He imagined the wonder they would feel at the new thing that here was already common.

He thought about the silk material that was traveling

along on chariots and on the backs of horses to villages that still labored under the heft and rub of hemp or wool or animal pelts, while silk had been in use elsewhere seemingly for a lifetime.

Would his marks for words do the same? Cangjie tried to imagine how the idea of writing would spread throughout the unified tribes under the Yellow Emperor. Who would carry the marks to those far lands? Who would teach the ideas that Cangjie had yet to create for himself?

He was jarred out of his thoughts when the driver stopped abruptly and pointed to a group of huts up on a hill. He was eager to see this farming invention, and his farewell with Cangjie was so brief that he had the horse moving before Cangjie had finished giving his thanks.

On the path up to the village, Cangjie again noticed so many more things, all the things of the earth, that would need marks to capture their words. He was hoping that a man who made his living with words, a poet, could help him conceive of a method to do so.

At the outskirts of the village, Cangjie envisioned again that moment he first understood how to capture the words, with unique prints and marks like the hoof of the dead animal.

He had been sick, but in that moment the solution came to him, he had witnessed spirits writhing out of the mud, shrieking in horror. It had seemed so real.

Was it real, in fact? In the years to come, would they put that in the story they mark down about Cangjie?

And what was it that the ghosts had to fear from this new invention that Cangjie felt so close to making?

Perhaps the poet could tell him.

It did not take long to find the poet when he arrived at the village. There were children huddled around him, laughing at a tale he spun. The children's laughter sounded like a group of hens running from a snake, yet it was a sound of joy. The poet's voice moved high and low like a song, in perfect time with the children's laughter.

Cangjie thought about how the poet was very like a musician. His words, his voice and his audience were together the poet's instrument. He was too far away to hear the words of the poet's tale, only the music of it. Cangjie listened longer and longer.

After a time, something fit into place between his ear and mind. Cangjie recognized that voice. It was his great friend, Wei. A thrill as he had not felt in ages raced up his backbone. If ever there was a poet who could help Cangjie create marks for words, it was the greatest poet of the age.

Eventually the children dispersed, a few of them putting a root vegetable or small charm in Wei's waiting hands. He smiled at them all as they left, and Cangjie saw his smile widen and brighten as their eyes met.

"My friend, it seems your audience does not compensate you so well," Cangjie said, looking at the collected items in Wei's hands.

"Alas, no. Children do not know the value of a

poem. They think the world is full of great ones in every crevice. But they will tell their parents what they heard, and the parents will come. Parents pay better." He smiled and put his bounty in a satchel at his side. "Why do I keep running into you in these strange places of my travels, Master Cangjie?"

"I am still in search of a way to complete my task for the Yellow Emperor."

"Ah, I see," said Wei. "I suspect you may be burdened by this task until your last breath. For words are as temporary and confusing and futile as life itself, I'm afraid."

"Great Wei, will you walk with me?" Cangjie asked. They went through the village and down to a vista overlooking the hill Cangjie had just climbed. Along its bottom ran a river that Cangjie watched for a few moments before he had the courage to tell Wei of his progress at his task for the Yellow Emperor.

Cangjie spoke of the inventions he had seen—the horse cart, silk, farming. He explained with his futile words why it was nevertheless important to trap words. He explained to his old friend, the great poet, how useful writing would be for everyone in the land, how it would alter the world as they knew it.

Then, with a deep breath to steady himself, he told Wei of his revelation in the rain—the hoof print and the wailing ghosts and the idea of a print or mark to equate to every thing in the earth and the heavens.

When he finished his story, Wei looked out at the downslope of the hill for a long time without speaking any words. He finally spoke, but with a music much sadder than Cangjie had ever heard the poet use.

"Master Cangjie, you have done it. You will succeed at what I thought impossible, and will capture words for all time."

Wei sighed and slumped forward. He began to cry.

"You will create a new world with your invention. Yet your invention will destroy the world, too, and me, and my poetry."

The great poet stood up and walked away quickly into the thick underbrush that grew uphill from the river. Cangjie stood and chased after him, but the branches and thorns caught on his silk robes and he could not keep up.

"Wei! Master Wei!" he called. But the poet did not stop. Cangjie took a great time extracting himself from the underbrush. When he was finally free, he waited there on the top edge of the slope for his old friend, until it began to grow dark. Cangjie headed into the village to find a host who would provide him with shelter, hoping to see Wei there.

He kept hearing the poet's words. *Yet your invention will destroy the world, too.*

The children in the hut where Cangjie found shelter for the night woke him early in the morning. They scampered across where he slept on the floor, moving quickly to see what the noise was out in the village street.

Cangjie sat up in fright at their high squeals and thunderous footfalls. It was still early, but he was surprised at how bright the day already was. And he listened to the growing noise outside the home where he had been graciously accepted.

Again, he had to slip away without giving his proper thanks. But the noise from the streets was too great to resist. There were too many words, too many ideas he might need to finish his task. He must find just one last secret, the way to make the marks. Anything in the wide world could give him that secret. So he slipped out of the house and joined a crowd that was gradually growing as the villagers arose with the sun to tend to their animals and move to the woods for water and hunting.

Everyone in the crowd was talking with someone. Cangjie hurried toward it to listen in. The villagers were saying to each other that it was to be the greatest poem of all time. It would be the one and only time anyone would ever hear it in the entire time of the earth. They would be the only villagers to receive the wisdom of the greatest poem, recited by the land's greatest poet.

Cangjie heard this from every conversation he listened in on. No matter how many times he heard it, he could not understand what it meant.

The greatest poem, only heard once?

Poetry was made for repeating, for telling the story with music and rhythm, putting it to memory so it never gets forgotten—wasn't that what Wei had told him many years ago?

It was then that Wei appeared from behind a nearby hut. The crowd cheered him and jittered with excitement at his approach. Wei carried his wooden box, which he stood upon to deliver his poems from a small height above the audience.

"My friends," Wei said without getting up on the box, "your village is most beautiful and welcoming. Yet for the greatest poem that will ever be uttered, we must leave it. Please follow me down to the river."

And with that, Wei made his way to the path that led downhill. Like obedient children, all of the villagers followed the poet along the path. Everyone gathered at the clearing along the river where the path ended, and formed a group before Wei who stood on his box with his back to the water.

Cangjie stood in the rear of the audience, his mind

racing at his old friend's stunt. There was a fire forming in Cangjie's belly, for surely this had something to do with their conversation yesterday about capturing the words. Was he trying to tell Cangjie that poetry would never die? Had he changed his thinking, and was now reciting a poem which said how marks for words would increase the place of poetry? That was Cangjie's hope, and he clung to it.

Whatever his intentions, word of Wei's greatest poem would travel fast from village to village, with the spectacle he was already creating, whether words were captured about the moment or not.

With a motion of the poet's arms, the crowd silenced.

Wei began his poem, in his masterful voice of words in song. Cangjie listened closely, and it did seem to be a poem greater than any other he had ever heard.

Yet no matter how hard he tried to still his mind and listen, Cangjie could not keep up with the poet's words. His thoughts kept floating to what blanketed his mind—the marks, the hoof print, the way to make a symbol for all things, that all people can make and recognize. There must be a simple way to capture words in marks.

Cangjie listened to the music of his old friend's voice without really hearing the words. He watched the villagers' faces as they heard the poem.

Words have such power, Cangjie thought. Even though these words last only for the briefest of moments, going from Wei's throat to the ears and minds of all the villagers, words carry the greatest power.

If only he could see the way to make the marks for words, then words would carry an even greater power.

Cangjie only heard a few words from Wei's poem. "Roots deep in earth," said one line. "The world births itself," said another. But he did not know what it meant. It was enough to witness the villagers hanging on every word, just to see how powerful words could be.

Then Wei changed everything. As he continued reciting his poem, Wei stepped down off his box and began walking backward into the water. The river was high, swollen from the enormous rainstorm that had soaked Cangjie to his bones. It rushed fast around Wei's ankles. Cangjie noticed the thick tree limbs and tufts of earth that churned in it.

Cangjie hung on every word of the poem that Wei shouted.

"In the old world,
the poet lived longest.
The poet's words lived full lives.
His words stayed alive when
the poet's body was gone.
In the old world this was true.
But now the old world dies.
So like a river carries water
always away,
Now the words will not stay.
Now the poet dies, too."

Wei was shouting over the noise of the flowing water, and Cangjie felt his heart explode in horror as Wei wrapped his arms around himself, and closed his eyes, and leaned back into the river's fast flow.

Shouts and gasps came from all the villagers. Cangjie and a few other men raced into the water to try to save him, but it was too late. They could only watch as Wei's bare feet rolled over above the surface, as his robe flapped up like the fin of a great fish, then as his back bobbed up for a long time before gradually sinking below the surface as his body drifted away.

After many moments of silence and shock, where there were no words but only the hushing sound of the river passing, the villagers began to talk to each other, and turn back toward the hill up to their huts, returning to their lives and responsibilities. For, Cangjie understood, what else could they do? The poet was dead, traveled far along now. There were chores to do and bodies to feed as they talked over what they'd just seen.

And there would grow from this day the strange story that the village would tell itself for many years, of the traveling poet who said a poem so wondrous that it dragged him into the river. Perhaps someday the river would come to be named after Wei.

Cangjie did not go up to the village. He stayed there on the riverbank, sitting on Wei's box, haunted by what had happened. What were the words of the poem? Cangjie hadn't listened enough, and those words were gone forever.

He stayed down by the riverside all day. He'd seen death many times, young men in the great battles, the old in his own village, men and animals along the roads in his travels. But he had never thought that he would cause the death of a great friend with the Yellow Emperor's mission.

In his worry over how there would ever be enough marks for all the words, Cangjie hadn't thought about whether he should even make the marks at all.

Perhaps failing at his task would be the best thing Cangjie could do for the world.

Cangjie closed his eyes and cried. For his great friend Wei, for the years he missed of his son's childhood, for the old world, for his beautiful wife, for his servants he never wished for, for the old legends yet to be captured of battles and dragons and gods and giants, for the Yellow Emperor and the new world of chariots and farming and silk robes, for all the marks he was to make and now perhaps would not.

He cried until he was out of tears and his throat was parched. He was exhausted and so tired of the task that had burdened him for so long.

When he opened his eyes, the day had grown bright. It was a glorious early winter day, the air clear and cold, the trees and animals readying for the long season to come. Nature had no idea of the tragedy she had just aided in. Nature did not see such things as tragedy at all, only natural.

Cangjie looked at the natural things all around him

where he sat on Wei's box. A little ways beside him, there was a wide expanse of grassless mud where the rainwater had swelled the river before it receded back inside its banks. There had been so much water that the worms and bugs were surfacing from beneath the earth, and two birds had found them. The birds raced to and fro, picking at the mud, leaving intricate trails of markings with their feet in the mud flat.

Cangjie stared at the footprints for a long time, until they no longer resembled footprints at all.

He looked at the ways the prints crossed each other to form new variations on the mark.

They looked like brush strokes.

Tiny, delicate, intricate brush strokes. Each one unique.

Cangjie was staring at the last secret. This was the answer to making marks. He had it, then. He felt the answer as firmly as he could imagine the feeling of a paintbrush in his hand.

This was how mankind could make prints for all words.

Small paintings for each word. A particular pattern of brush strokes as a symbol to make a mark for every thing.

It was a simple and elegant solution. He knew it would work.

Cangjie had invented writing.

It was the saddest moment of his life.

Winter came quickly. Cangjie spent the cold months there in the village above the riverbank where he had seen the bird footprints in the mud. He made no friends, shared few words with any of the villagers.

In the name of the Yellow Emperor and the decree he was following, Cangjie commandeered the hut of an old man who had recently died and lived within it like a crazed hermit.

All he did was make the marks. A mark for every thing.

Cangjie created the characters of writing.

He pulled out strands of his hair and knotted them to stiff twigs he collected in the woods.

He cut the hairs into lengths like that of a painter's brush.

When an animal was slaughtered, Cangjie collected the blood in a bowl and used it as paint to create the characters. He brushed each one on anything he could find—the dried skin of a slaughtered pig, a flat face of a split tree limb, light-colored blankets and robes.

When the blood ran out, Cangjie demanded a knife from a hunter in the name of the Yellow Emperor and carved his marks into hard surfaces—emptied tortoise shells, or the shoulder and hip bones of slaughtered animals.

The cold months passed and Cangjie's hut began to fill with surfaces covered in more and more characters. He worked, barely eating, hardly registering any emotion. He knew he must stop before he filled the hut with characters and suffocated himself. But still he recorded words.

Finally, when the ice atop the river cracked and tiny green shoots came out of the ground, Cangjie began to come to life again, too. The earth had begun to birth itself all over again. So must he.

Cangjie hired many horse carts in the village and promised them riches when they arrived at the Yellow Emperor's palace. He traveled with them to the Yellow Emperor in a great rush, the bones and tree limbs and tortoise shells and rock faces, everything he'd recorded a word on, all rattling and rustling in the cart beds like a great commotion of village gossip.

When they arrived at the gate to the city walls, the guards did not want to let them pass.

"You are no envoys of the Yellow Emperor," they said. "You are peddlers of trash. Be on your way."

Cangjie insisted. "This is not junk. I have words captured here in our carts."

"Pffft! Such a thing is not possible," said the guard.

With much pleading, Cangjie convinced him to send a messenger to the Yellow Emperor. After some time, the messenger returned leading a long train of servants and attendants, and the Emperor's wife Leizu, and finally the Yellow Emperor himself, wearing his bright silk robe.

Leizu made her way to the front of the line quickly.

"Master Cangjie! It has been so long since we have seen you! We have been waiting eagerly for your return for many months and are overjoyed that you are here now." She bowed to him.

Cangjie did not expect to be bowed to. For so long he had been lost in his world of words and marks that he had almost forgotten how to communicate in the human world. It took him several seconds to understand what had happened, and when he did, he quickly returned the bow, bending deeply and wrenching his back.

The voice of the Yellow Emperor rang out from back in the line.

"Step aside, Guard! Let in the man that will change the world. Master Cangjie! You are welcome to this palace!"

They returned to the very room where the Yellow Emperor had charged Cangjie with this task. The Yellow Emperor sat patiently beside his beautiful wife in their silk robes, with a throng of close advisors standing behind them, and a great deal of curious palace workers who heard that Cangjie had trapped words, as if they were birds in a net.

The Yellow Emperor asked of Cangjie's success, and Cangjie told him everything he had seen, right up to the moment when the birds made their impressions in the mud.

Cangjie then pointed at each mark he had made, explaining each in detail, holding up tree limbs, scraps of old robes, flat rocks, and decoding how the mark was unique and represented only that word. Cangjie had presented a small portion of his marks when he noticed the Emperor eyeing the tall piles of objects covered in Cangjie's bloody marks and carvings.

As Cangjie paused for a gourd of water, ready to explain the next items, the Yellow Emperor stood.

"My subjects, when I gave Master Cangjie this task, I could only guess what I meant. I did not know it was possible. Master Cangjie, you have surpassed even my wildest dreams of success. Forever after, you shall be known for this feat you have done. And for as long as you live, you shall be rewarded for it. I shall make this work known across the land."

And with that, he stood, hiding a yawn behind the drooping cuff of his silk robe, and left for his chambers.

That night, the Yellow Emperor threw a great feast, as raucous as his own wedding reception. For though the world had not yet changed, the Yellow Emperor knew that it would, as the idea spread among the united tribes.

The morning after the feast, Cangjie heard a knock on his door. He was still in bed and did not answer, but the door opened anyway. Eleven attendants streamed in, followed by the Emperor's wife. Cangjie was shocked and embarrassed, and pulled the silk bedding around him.

Yet the Emperor's wife did not show any embarrassment. She walked to where he slept and handed him a very fine portion of dried pig's skin and a brush and a bowl of paint like liquid silk.

"Master Cangjie," she bowed. Cangjie did the best bow he could manage from his bed.

"Master Cangjie, you are to use this to put down marks for your wife, telling her of your success here at the palace, and of your love for her. And you are to invite her to join you here with great haste. You will teach these characters to Shen, our greatest messenger, and he will deliver this message of marks."

She bowed again and left before Cangjie could reply. He cried for a long time before he was able to get up and, with great care, make the marks for his wife.

As the message traveled, Cangjie went each day to his workroom. Palace servants brought Cangjie finely-woven material that artists would have used for painting, and he was to copy each character onto these with the fine paint used by palace artists. For weeks, he worked. When the material ran out, they brought him dried fronds, and when these ran out, they brought him long planks of dried wood.

As he copied, the Yellow Emperor summoned the most respected premiers and greatest poets from each of the tribes across all the distant lands. Upon their arrival, Cangjie taught them all the characters he had created. The more he taught them, the more he understood that there were many, many more characters to create. The work of writing would never be finished.

The premiers sat in astonishment at first, then watched with great attention, then gradually grew tired. They each instructed their attendants to pay strict attention and teach them later.

After several days, it was just Cangjie and the attendants in the room.

But no matter. In a few moons, his wife would arrive at the palace and all would be well.

Cangjie went on teaching the marks, as if there would always be more to teach.

Afterword

The earth spins in the same orbit as ever, yet with each revolution it returns as an entirely new world of ideas.

Cangjie and his wife saw this when they finally left the Yellow Emperor's palace. They retreated to the great palace that the Emperor had built for them along the banks of the Wei River where Cangjie had invented writing.

Shoyu and his many wives also came to live in his parents' palace. Cangjie's son farmed great fields in the rich soil along the river. Cangjie and his wife ate well from the fruits of the land and their son's labor.

And messengers arrived each day, carrying writings and decrees and news. The messengers now read from scrolls or planks rather than reciting from memory.

The Yellow Emperor continued to change the world. He divided the seasons into tiny units called days and added them into a cycle called a calendar. He devised a way for wild animals to live in villages and follow commands. One of his concubines invented a way to eat by picking up food with two small, straight sticks.

Occasionally, the messengers would read the old stories. Each time, the Yellow Emperor became more and more grand. He beheaded a thousand men with one stroke of his sword at the Battle of Zhuolu, one said. Chi You, the Yellow Emperor's rival in the battle, now had the legs of lions and a bronze head.

One day, Cangjie returned to the palace where his wife rested. He laughed so loudly that the servants came running, thinking he suffered from a great sadness.

He found his wife on their luxurious bed, resting. Her limbs had grown weak and her skin was loose. Cangjie still thought her the most beautiful woman on the earth.

"Dearest," he laughed. "I have just heard the latest story about the old times, and to my surprise, it was about me!"

"Oh?" she said, raising an eyebrow.

"I am even greater than I ever knew," Cangjie said. "Such vision I have! The stories say there are four eyes upon my forehead."

Cangjie and his wife laughed for a long time, then rested. This is how they spent much of their last years together, laughing at the new ideas that came to them in words.

For they knew the story of how writing changed the world.

They understood that was how the world is always changed.

Idea by idea.

Story by story.

Word by word.

ABOUT THE AUTHOR

Baker Lawley is a lifelong storyteller, as a journalist, a magazine and book editor, and professor of creative writing—and also as a septic system tester, a lifeguard, a movie theater janitor, and a school uniform salesman.

Baker lives in Minneapolis with his wife and daughter and their lazy hound dog.

Get free ebooks when you sign up for Baker's newsletter! Visit www.bakerlawley.com/contact. You'll also get special offers, updates, and upcoming book release news!

You can also follow Baker on the web:

Tumblr - http://blog.bakerlawley.com

Facebook - www.facebook.com/BakerLawleyAuthor

Twitter - @bakerlawley

Email - baker@bakerlawley.com.

Would you be willing to review this book?

Thank you for reading my work. I would be honored if you would give it an honest review on Amazon or Barnes and Noble, on your website or blog, or anywhere else.

Word of mouth is still the best way books are sold, so please tell your friends and other readers about it on social media—or in person! As an author, I really appreciate your help in spreading the word about my work.

Thank you, always, for reading.

Also available from Baker Lawley

~~~

THE BATTLE HYMN BLUES

Stoney Nix can play anything, from Beethoven to the Blues, on his old rattletrap piano. It's just a gift, and a good one. Music is his ticket out of Pinewood, Alabama, his ironic, dying hometown, where they reenact the Civil War but cancel marching band because it's too small. Then Sadie Green, the hilarious and beautiful new girl (and Stoney's major crush), convinces him to fight in the fake Civil War battle.

What happens there will haunt Stoney forever—and only through voices of the past, struggle, friendship, and his music, will Stoney find himself.

* * *
~~~

This Is The Play

Book 1 in the *Such Sweet Sorrow Trilogy*

Lewis Champion is in love-total, hopeless, unrequited love-with Jubilee Marshfield. Which is complicated, because she's his best friend. He can't find the courage to tell her since he's a wallflower. Watching people, making theories, never acting on his feelings.

But when Lewis' awesome grandfather, Paps, dies, the will contains the strangest request of Lewis. And what he must face, with his friends alongside him, gives new meaning to the idea of "acting."

Visit www.bakerlawley.com/books to read an excerpt and get your copy!

A Good Idea at the Time

A collection of six raucous short stories about growing up—starring a vagabond uncle hellbent on corrupting his nephew, and a jazz musician stuck in a saxophone factory, and a crew of regulars watching their town take away their bar, just to name a few.

Full of hilarious moments, melancholy, great characters and that signature voice that award-winning author Baker Lawley is known for, *A Good Idea at the Time* has something every reader will love.

Visit www.bakerlawley.com/books to read an excerpt and get your copy!

All books available from Baker Lawley:

The Battle Hymn Blues
This Is The Play (Such Sweet Sorrow Trilogy: Book One)
The Man Who Invented Writing
A Good Idea at The Time: Stories
297 Story Ideas for Writing Novels and Short Fiction
Tracks
No Jazz in Indiana
Regulars
Funeral Games

Visit www.bakerlawley.com for reading excerpts and links to purchase.
Sign up for the newsletter and receive free ebooks!

www.ingramcontent.com/pod-product-compliance
Lightning Source LLC
LaVergne TN
LVHW090956080826
845145LV00003B/1028

* 9 7 8 0 6 1 5 7 2 4 1 4 0 *